ALSO BY KEVIN WIGNALL

For the Dogs

People Die

WHO IS CONRAD HIRST?

KEVIN WIGNALL

SIMON & SCHUSTER PAPERBACKS

NEW YORK   TORONTO   LONDON   SYDNEY

SIMON & SCHUSTER
Rockefeller Center
1230 Avenue of the Americas
New York, NY 10020

This book is a work of fiction. Names, characters, places, and incidents either are products of the author's imagination or are used fictitiously. Any resemblance to actual events or locales or persons, living or dead, is entirely coincidental.

Copyright © 2007 by Kevin Wignall

All rights reserved, including the right to reproduce this book or portions thereof in any form whatsoever. For information, address Simon & Schuster Subsidiary Rights Department, 1230 Avenue of the Americas, New York, NY 10020.

First Simon & Schuster trade paperback edition November 2007

SIMON & SCHUSTER and colophon are registered trademarks of Simon & Schuster, Inc.

For information about special discounts for bulk purchases,
please contact Simon & Schuster Special Sales at
1-800-456-6798 or business@simonandschuster.com.

Designed by Karolina Harris

Manufactured in the United States of America

10 9 8 7 6 5 4 3 2 1

Library of Congress Cataloging-in-Publication Data
Wignall, Kevin.
  Who is Conrad Hirst? / Kevin Wignall.
    p. cm.
  1. Murder for hire—Fiction. 2. Revenge—Fiction. I. Title.

PR6123.I36W47 2007
823'.92—dc22

2007015595

ISBN-13: 978-1-4165-4072-4
ISBN-10:   1-4165-4072-5

For N, A, and R.
Who are you?

Acknowledgments

MANY thanks, as ever, to David Rosenthal, my publisher at Simon & Schuster. Equal gratitude for her advice and support goes to my excellent new editor, Kerri Kolen. And I consider myself very lucky to have the services of three superb agents, Jonny Geller in London, Deborah Schneider in New York, and Justin Manask in Los Angeles.

Beyond that, there are too many to thank by name among those who helped during the writing of this book or who played some small part in the various events that inspired it, but you'll know if you were there. Not everyone rode in the cable car, but we all saw the light.

WHO IS CONRAD HIRST?

Conrad Hirst

Dear Anneke,

I should have written to you like this ten years ago and I should have kept writing. The night I found out you were dead, I should have run back to the house and started writing and never stopped. But I ran the wrong way, I never put that loss into words, and all the horrors of the last decade, all the murders—yes, I'm a murderer now, many times over—all of it arose, in one way or another, from that failure.

I can imagine you remonstrating with me, telling me that it was a war zone, that similar horrors befell many of the people who were foolish or unfortunate enough to be in Yugoslavia at that time. It's true, the shells that fell on you in the market square also fell on countless others, and I was not the only one to get caught up in the fighting, to cross over from observer to participant in the squalid chaos that reigned there.

And I have no doubt that I was scarred by the things I did and saw, but none of it, none of what happened to me excuses my failure to get help and leave that violence behind.

None of it excuses my betrayal of the person you knew and everything he stood for.

Think of that person, the English boy who wanted to be a photographer—he was kind, wasn't he, and gentle and funny? Do you remember him? Then you should hate him, because for the past nine years that same person has been a professional killer, working for a German crime boss, killing people for money he didn't need, remorseless, empty of any kindness at all.

The most recent was only yesterday afternoon in Chur. Yes, yesterday afternoon I killed a seventy-six-year-old man called Hans Klemperer. I don't know why they wanted him dead, and at the time I didn't care. To me, he was no more than a set of instructions, his death no more important a detail than the destruction of his computer.

Now, though, now I feel bad for the first time in ten years, a gnawing discomfort in the knowledge of what I've done. Call it conscience, if you will; all I know is that it's a sadness for which I'm profoundly grateful, no less than if my sight had been restored to me after years of blindness. What overtook me yesterday was a longing to be the person I once was.

I've already changed, and I swear Klemperer is the last man I'll kill for money. I can't promise not to kill again, not yet—I wish I could, but I've thought it through endlessly over the last twenty-four hours, and of necessity there are still four more murders I have to commit, four more deaths that lie between me and the person I was on the day you died. Of course, in many respects, I'll never be that person again, but this is my opportunity to at least end the sickness.

If there were another way, if I could start afresh without killing another person, I'd take that path, because I see now what I always should have seen, that it's what you would have wanted me to do, what we would have wanted. As it is, four more deaths will count for nothing in the context of what I've done—they'll bear no more significance than the burning of this letter a few minutes from now.

What matters, surely, is that I've written this letter! The process has started, and there'll be no turning back. In some perverse way, I did the things I did in the last ten years because I lost you. Perhaps you'll think it equally perverse, but these final four killings, everything I'm about to do, it's all because I loved you, because I still love you, and because I always will.

Conrad

1

THE snow had smothered the town, not with the deep drifts that would come and go through the Bavarian winter, but enough to give the evening a sense of enclosed stillness. Between snow and lights there was a comforting glow around the houses. Even Frank's house, a brutal 1970s chalet that Conrad had never liked, looked picturesque in its winter clothes.

Yet as soon as he got out of the car, Conrad was drawn from the houses around him to the half-hidden view of the mountain above, its trees and slopes and outcrops all dusted in shadowy blue light. The cable car station was lost in the clouds and the dense thickets of lazily falling snow, but the knowledge that it was up there was soothing, maybe for no other reason than that it reminded him of the distant past, a time when he might still have been able to turn back, before the irreparable damage had been done.

For a minute or two he didn't want to move and surrender this peace. He didn't want to spend time with Frank and he didn't want the dream of the last two weeks to be snatched away from him, for Frank to tell him that he'd miscalculated, that escaping this business would not be so easy.

He'd been a ghost, that was the fact at the center of his plans, a fact that he'd convinced himself of, and as long as he stood out there in the clean coldness of early evening, he could hold onto it and believe it true. The trouble was, he'd remain a ghost unless he confronted whatever alternate truth Frank might have to offer him.

Even if there were more than four, even if every crime boss and police force in Europe knew about him, he needed to hear it. He liked the cool simplicity of killing his way out of the business, but if the facts suggested that it would be impossible, he was still determined to find another way, whatever it took.

He followed the vague line of the path that was still showing through the snow and knocked on the door. Frank opened it almost immediately, took the briefest moment to place him, and then beamed a smile, pointing at Conrad with both hands like they'd once been in a band together.

"Hey, man! This is unexpected," he said in his West Coast surfer accent.

He almost felt sorry for Frank. He was over fifty now, his stockiness running to fat a little, but he was squeezed into clothes designed for skinny kids half his age, and his short hair was dyed a yellowy blond, a high-maintenance operation that only served to make him look even older than he was. He could imagine Frank being offended by every deeply etched line in his own perma-tanned face, like they were all personal betrayals.

"Good to see you, Frank."

As if double-checking against his own knowledge, Frank said, "You're not on a job?"

Conrad laughed. "Did you send me on a job?" Frank shrugged and looked scatterbrained, a goofy act he'd perfected over the years, one that belied the dangerous truth, the early years in some elite U.S. Army regiment, the two decades as one of the operational hubs around which Eberhardt's criminal empire revolved. "I've been away for a couple of days, thought I'd call in—I need to pick your brain about something."

There was that look again, hinting that there wasn't much to pick, but he stepped back and said, "Come on in. You hungry?"

"No, thanks," said Conrad as Frank shut the door behind him. He walked into the sitting room, took his coat off, and put it on one of the sofas.

"Port wine?"

"Sure, I'll have a glass of port with you."

Conrad sat on the sofa next to his coat. Frank poured two glasses of port, handed one to Conrad and sat on the opposite sofa. The fireplace between them was loaded with logs but Conrad had never seen it lit—perhaps just as well, because the room was already suffocating under the blanket of central heating. Even so, a crackling fire would have been a nice touch for two old colleagues of sorts, looking back on their decade's acquaintance.

Conrad sipped at his port and nodded appreciatively, but before he could comment aloud, Frank said, "So what's on your mind, Conrad?"

"I'm thinking about quitting."

He'd said the words and it was done now. Even if he changed his mind immediately, they'd have him marked as potentially volatile, someone who might become a liability or a threat further down the road. With those four words he'd started a process that, in one way or another, could not be stopped. The challenge now was to keep himself moving and hold the advantage.

"I didn't know you smoked." Frank looked sheepish, an admission that it hadn't been funny; maybe a realization, too, that Conrad wasn't much of a foil for witty banter. "Seriously, that'd be a shame, not least because you're good. But you know, I'll guarantee this has something to do with turning thirty—everyone has a wobble at thirty."

"I'm thirty-two. Anyway, that's not it. I just want to do something different with my life. I can't do this anymore."

"Have you been reading Charles Handy?" Conrad looked baffled by way of response. "You know, the business guru? *The Empty Raincoat*? This whole idea of the multicareer life."

On several occasions in the past, at times like this, he'd wondered if Frank was a junkie of some sort—prescription drugs, that kind of thing—but he knew it was an act, that a person couldn't do Frank's job without being mentally above water. This was just one of Frank's games, and Conrad knew he had to play along to get to what he wanted.

"Frank, what are you talking about?"

"I guess that's a 'no'." Then Frank sprang his little verbal ambush and was pleased with himself, like he was a dazzling trial lawyer working a witness. "So, would this have anything to do with killing a certain old man in Chur two weeks ago?"

Conrad smiled, thinking back to Chur, to the sun shining on the cafés in the square. As unusual as this snowfall was for early November, it was nothing compared to the Indian summer they'd experienced two weeks before.

Frank took Conrad's smile as an admission and said, "At

least you killed him. But I'll be straight, I never dreamed he'd get to you. He was a wily old bastard, a talker, but I never dreamed he'd get to you."

"It wasn't Klemperer, as such. Something did happen in Chur, but . . . I just had a moment of clarity, you know? I can't do this anymore." Frank looked troubled, possibly by the logistics of replacing him, possibly by something more sinister, but either way, Conrad was eager to move on now. "Changing the subject, I was thinking of all the people I've dealt with over the last ten years, all the people who know what I've done, who I am." He laughed as he added, "All the people who could pick me out of a lineup."

"And?" Frank seemed genuinely intrigued by the shift in the conversation.

"It's amazing really—Brodsky, Carrington, Deschamp, Steiner . . ."

"Who's Steiner?"

"The guy I first worked with for you."

"Schmidt," said Frank, correcting him.

"Of course. I don't know why I thought it was Steiner. Anyway, he's dead, just like all the others, just like Lewis Jones."

"You're an unlucky guy to be around," said Frank, smiling, seeing this list of names as some sort of humorous parlor game.

"Or it's a line of work with a very brief life expectancy. By my reckoning, the only people in the business who know me and are still alive are Julius Eberhardt, Freddie Fischer, and Fabio Gaddi."

There they were, all introduced to him by Frank back in the early days—Eberhardt, his employer; Fischer, who supplied him with arms; Gaddi, who provided documents when he needed them. He didn't know if Fischer and Gaddi worked for Eberhardt or if they were independent operatives—he'd never needed to know and had never been curious.

He'd dealt with them only as they'd related to him and he'd deal with them in the weeks ahead on the same basis. They'd been his world for nine years, a closed and claustrophobic world that he was about to dismantle piece by piece.

"When did you meet Gaddi?"

"I didn't, but we've spoken on the phone, and the guy makes my passports and papers—I'd say that counts as knowing me."

Frank seemed to take the facts in now, and said, "You're right, that really is amazing. But then, that's why we always liked you—you make yourself invisible."

"So you agree, you can't think of anyone else?" Frank shook his head questioningly, clearly wondering where this was going. "Don't you get it, Frank? It means I can start afresh and never worry about this world coming back to haunt me."

Frank looked suddenly troubled and said, "You're serious about this? About quitting?" Conrad nodded, causing Frank to look even more uneasy. Hesitantly, he said, "Look, Conrad, it might not be as straightforward as all that. You have to understand the underbelly of this business—it's more complicated than it seems. What I mean is, getting out isn't always as simple as saying 'I quit.'"

Conrad realized Frank hadn't been taking him seriously, that Frank had really believed he was experiencing nothing more than a "wobble." Now, too late, he was trying to hint at some labyrinthine structure that was hard to escape.

He was missing the point, of course, because the complexity of Eberhardt's empire, and the criminal underworld that it was a part of, was irrelevant when set against the simple fact that Frank had already confirmed: Conrad didn't have to find his way out of the labyrinth, just punch his way through four walls.

"Do more than those three people know who I am?"

He looked pained as he said, "No, that's not what I'm saying."

"What you're saying doesn't matter. I've killed a lot of people in ten years, Frank. Killing a few more to get out of the business seems like a good equation to me. The way I see it, the underbelly of the business counts for nothing if no one's alive who can connect me to it."

Frank seemed to take a moment to catch up, then looked askance at Conrad and said, "You've got to be joking, of course." He was smiling, relaxed, but his tone was vaguely threatening, maybe because he understood that there were four people in the frame, not three. "Okay, just hypothetically, say you were crazy enough to go down this route, and I don't think you are, Conrad, not by a long way, but say you were, how would you get Eberhardt?"

Conrad smiled to himself, because he knew he'd calculated correctly. If Eberhardt's security was the only obstacle Frank could come up with, he was as good as free. He'd never thought any of the killings themselves would present a problem; his only concern had been the possibility of being known by people he'd never actually dealt with.

"It's funny I couldn't remember Schmidt's name because I've always remembered something he told me, something about the one constant weak spot in Eberhardt's security. You do remember that Schmidt was one of his bodyguards for a while?" Frank looked unimpressed, waiting for something more substantial. "The country estate near Birkenstein."

"I've been there many times," said Frank with satisfaction, which in itself exposed how rattled he was. "Julius spends most of his time there, I know, and despite what Schmidt might have told you, it's probably the most secure private residence I've ever seen. I mean, don't get me wrong, Conrad, you're good in the sense that you're reliable, discreet, detached even—but you're not James Bond."

"Maybe I'm a little closer to James Bond than you think." The words sounded ridiculous, but he knew he had one over on Frank. "It's not the estate itself. Apparently, our friend Julius has a religious streak. Every Sunday that he's there, he goes to the chapel in the village, only two bodyguards, in a place that Schmidt told me is a sniper's paradise."

Frank nodded nonchalantly, though Conrad could see he'd surprised him. Frank then said, "I knew a couple of snipers way back when. Takes a lot of training and a very particular mind-set—not the same as killing a man at ten feet, not the same at all. It's not just a question of picking up an M24 off Freddie and hiding in a tree. So tell me, Conrad, where did you get your sniper training? I'm curious."

Conrad didn't bother to tell him he'd once known a sniper, too, in Yugoslavia, a guy he'd heard them call "Vasko." He remembered him, lean and sinewy but smiling a lot, an easy smile, and the muscles in one eye always itching toward a squint. He'd had no specialized training, only years of hunting in the hills, and yet if he could see it through his sights, he could shoot the cigarette out of a man's mouth. For all Conrad knew, Vasko had survived the war and was back hunting in the hills and forests that were his home.

"I don't plan on being a mile away, and I won't be relying on one shot."

"So you'd risk hitting innocent people," said Frank with a hint of completely unearned moral outrage. If it suited him, Frank would have blown up the whole church.

Conrad ignored him, not least because he'd long since lost the discernment necessary to tell an innocent person from a guilty one. "I'll drive to Birkenstein tonight, check the place out, do Freddie on the way home, get the hardware, hopefully do Eberhardt a week tomorrow, then Gaddi."

Frank shook his head, an expression of disbelief, but he was still acting as if he wasn't in danger himself. He knocked back his port and then looked down, contemplating the glass. Conrad guessed he was wondering if the time was coming to throw the glass, and in Frank's hands that could prove enough of a missile to give him the edge.

Conrad decided to head him off at the pass—he dipped his hand into his coat and pulled out his gun. Frank looked up, his eyes drawn by the movement, and was genuinely surprised to see the gun with its silencer already attached.

"I altered and strengthened the inside pocket. It's not perfect, but good for situations where you can't wear it or carry a bag."

"I'm not surprised by your tailoring, Conrad, I'm surprised that you're aiming a gun at me."

"It's nothing personal, Frank."

Frank looked derisively and said, "Oh spare me the clichés! Jesus, forget the madness a second, what about the disloyalty, what about stabbing people in the back, people who've helped you? You do remember that, don't you, Conrad? I took you in. You were a wreck, and I took you in and gave you a life."

13

Conrad nodded, acknowledging the point and inadvertently offering hope in response to Frank's indignation. He thought back to his arrival here nine years before, the spell its preternatural calm had cast on him. He'd booked into Die Alpenrose and hadn't wanted to leave, like a convalescent soldier from an earlier war.

In truth, Frank hadn't helped him at all; he'd merely smoothed the path of his descent. But Conrad couldn't help but feel grateful to him, and now that he was here, he understood in some detached way that this wasn't fair. Frank didn't deserve to die, and certainly not by Conrad's hand.

"I'm sorry, Frank, but you know who I am. There's nothing more to it than that." It sounded like a feeble excuse for killing someone, but he imagined he'd killed some of his targets for less over the years.

Frank tried a look of smug superiority, but it was undermined by his adrenaline jitters and he sounded slightly arch as he said, "Oh, *I* know who you are, but tell me, Conrad, are you absolutely sure *you* know who you are?"

"Nice try, Frank. I've been sick, I know that, but I remember everything I've done these ten years. That's the worst of it—I know all too well who I am."

"You're forgetting something . . ."

"I'm not forgetting anything."

The conversation was going nowhere. Conrad shot Frank in the chest, the bullet meeting his final words halfway. "I lied," said Frank, before the bullet punched him into the sofa and the glass fell to the floor.

He didn't die instantly, and, apart from the bloody hole in his chest, he looked like he could keep conversing all night.

Conrad couldn't resist asking, "What do you mean? What did you lie about?"

Frank's eyes looked left and right, as if he was struggling to see where the question had come from or what it meant. Then he seemed to spot Conrad sitting opposite and a sense of understanding crossed his face. He coughed a little, producing blood, his lungs rattling with fluid. "Everything," whispered Frank, almost to himself.

"I forgive you, Frank," said Conrad, and immediately felt it was a cheap shot to make fun of a dying man's words. He thought about adding something else, something more fitting, but Frank was done listening.

Conrad put the gun aside and sipped at his port, savoring the silence. He told himself it didn't matter if Frank had lied to him. He'd always kept his distance from the business anyway, and like he'd said, as long as there were only four people—three now—who could connect him with it, the lies he'd been told and the truths they concealed were of no importance.

Conrad finished his drink, then worked Frank's house the same way he'd been instructed to do the Klemperer job, killing the hard disk on his computer, collecting the loose disks. He took the SIM card from Frank's phone, too, then built a couple of bonfires, one in the study and one around Frank.

And as he walked back to the car, his footprints already being erased by the gently relentless fall of more snow, the sitting room window was beginning to glow orange. A new house would be built here, and the neighbors would be shocked but happy that Frank was gone.

They'd never taken to Frank. Conrad had wondered if it

was because he was American, or because his wife, who'd left Frank a couple of years before Conrad first met him, had been black. But he'd underestimated the good people of Mittenwald. They'd disliked Frank because they knew, as only people in a small town could know, that Frank was a lowlife.

As Conrad drove through the worsening weather toward Miesbach he sensed they were probably right. Maybe that was why he felt nothing for the man he'd killed. After Klemperer, he thought he'd feel something for every killing, particularly someone he'd known so long. But right now he felt as little for Frank as he did for all those victims whose names he could no longer even remember.

The only thing keeping Frank in his thoughts at all was a curiosity about those final words—that he'd lied, about everything. Conrad had already dismissed them once, and they'd probably been no more than a desperate play by a man who knew he was up against it.

But the words kept coming back to trouble him. He was driving to Miesbach, then south to Birkenstein. He'd check in late to his guesthouse, do his recon in the morning, and so on, and so on. He'd rehearsed it all in his head a hundred times in the last few days, but even the possibility of an unknown quantity was disturbing the rhythm of his thoughts.

What if he had been lied to? What if nothing was as it seemed? None of it would have concerned him two weeks ago, but the Klemperer job had changed everything—he understood that now. Perhaps for the first time ever, as much as Conrad tried to suppress it, he feared what he didn't know about the world, and most of all, he feared what he didn't know about himself.

2

CONRAD could see the brightness through the curtains but he didn't look out of the window until he'd finished dressing, and then he couldn't believe that he'd made it there the night before. Under a startling blue sky, the landscape was pillowed white, all its sharp edges and hard surfaces softened and lost in snow.

As a kid, a scene like that would have filled him with excitement and he would have been desperate to get out to the nearest slopes, badgering his parents to skip breakfast. He hadn't been skiing in a long time though, and couldn't find even the faint echo of that former enthusiasm.

It was just one more reason why he had to succeed with this. He was too young for so many things to be locked away in the past like forgotten keepsakes. Eberhardt was probably just a few miles away and he'd woken to the same beautiful morning, almost certainly untroubled, because there were people like Conrad to absorb trouble for him. It was an injustice he couldn't tolerate anymore—the cost was too high.

He went down to the breakfast room, which was surprisingly busy given that it was more or less between seasons. A group of two young couples sat at one table, talking animatedly. An elderly couple sat in the corner, sternly eating their eggs, and a middle-aged man sat on his own.

Conrad took a plate at the buffet and selected some meat and cheese and some of the heavy bread they seemed to favor in the mornings. As he was standing there, a middle-aged woman came in and started assembling her own breakfast plate.

She was dressed in walking clothes, as was the man sitting on his own, and for some reason, he imagined them both being retired schoolteachers. The woman tried to catch Conrad's eye a couple of times as they moved around each other, then managed it and said cheerily, "Grüß Gott!"

He guessed she was foreign, assuming that a Bavarian wouldn't have been on holiday here and that a non-Bavarian German wouldn't have used the local greeting. *"Grüß Gott,"* he said, politely distant.

It only encouraged her. *"Es ist ein schöner Tag,"* she said with a clearly noticeable Scottish accent. He gave her a half smile and turned away, and when he sat down he could hear her saying to her husband, the other walker, *"He's* not a Bavarian—far too rude."

He nodded, but looked like he was agreeing for the sake of it as he said, "Probably a Prussian. Very abrupt, the Prussians."

Conrad liked the fact that they thought he was German, and a Prussian at that—if he'd had a dueling scar he might have understood it. What he most preferred to give was no impression at all, but if he was going to register with strangers, a false impression was always a good fallback, a preposterous one even better. Anything other than people asking where in Dorset he'd grown up or where had he gone to college.

He ate his breakfast in peace, saved by his innate hostility. As he was finishing, the two couples got into a good-humored dispute over some issue of the day, talking over each other in clipped German accents. The Scots looked disapprovingly, perhaps understanding what was being said. But then one of the men laughed out some response that included the name "Eberhardt." His friends laughed but his wife immediately upbraided him, clearly stressing that he ought to be careful with what he said.

As Conrad left, he imagined she'd been concerned about causing offense to people who might know Eberhardt. But if it was something else, if she'd read enough about him to know how dangerous he was, she could hardly have known that the brutal underbelly of his empire had been sitting a few feet away eating breakfast with them.

He strolled through the wood-paneled lobby where a man of about his own age was standing behind the desk. He smiled as Conrad appeared and said, "Ah, Mr. Hirst, I'm sorry I didn't have an opportunity to meet you last night. I'm Herr Sattler."

He was wearing a traditional felt tunic and his brown hair looked suspiciously blow-dried, but he was young, much younger than Conrad had imagined. "I'm sorry, I expected you to be . . ."

"Older," suggested Sattler, smiling. "Many people have said this. My e-mails make me sound old, it seems. I have to work on them."

"Not at all," said Conrad and shook his hand.

"So, what brings you to us, Mr. Hirst?" He added in a playfully chastising tone, "And for one night only!"

"I'm breaking the journey from Salzburg back to Luxembourg, and don't worry, hopefully, next time I'll bring my wife and we can stay for a few days."

The explanation for his current stay had been received blankly, but Sattler looked pleased by the mention of the fictitious wife and the plans for future visits. Equally though, it could have been part of an act, because he said, "And what is your line of business, Mr. Hirst, if you don't mind me asking?"

This was all he needed, a curious, possibly even suspicious hotelier. He could only assume they had few lone guests and were too far off the main routes for passing trade. "I don't mind you asking at all, Herr Sattler, but I'm a little curious as to why you would want to know—my line of business isn't very exciting."

Sattler smiled and laughed to himself and was apologetic as he said, "You must forgive me, but we don't have many single English gentlemen staying here, but occasionally, you know, we have journalists." Conrad feigned confusion, but he could see what was troubling Sattler now. Eberhardt attracted the press, and maybe others besides, and for whatever reason—distaste, loyalty, pressure from the man himself—Herr Sattler didn't like those kinds of guests. "There is a local resident who is quite . . ."

"Famous?"

"No. I think, controversial. He's an important figure in the community here, but the newspapers and magazines, sometimes they send people making stories."

Conrad shook his head, a show of being baffled as he

said, "Who is this person? Would I have heard of him?"

"I don't think so. He's just a businessman, but you know, here in Bavaria, in Germany, we take business very seriously."

"That's what I like about the Germans," said Conrad, but Sattler clearly wasn't sure whether he was being genuine or not. "And you needn't worry, I'm not a journalist. I'm afraid I'll also be leaving immediately after lunch."

"Of course." Sattler once again looked apologetic, as if he'd impugned Conrad's character by suggesting he was a journalist. As if to make up for the slight, he said, "So how will you spend your morning with us?"

"I'm just taking a walk down to the village. I want to look at the chapel—it's how I heard about Birkenstein."

Sattler was already backtracking, apparently ready to believe anything Conrad said now, even a lie about driving out of his way in a blizzard just to see a chapel. "Yes, it's very fine, but this is not a good day for walking. You have seen the snow." He thought about it for a second and said, "You ski? *Langlaufen*?"

"I do ski, but I've only skied cross-country once."

"So, like riding a bicycle. I lend you the skis."

The offer didn't sound open to negotiation and Conrad realized it would probably make his task easier, so he smiled and said, "That's very kind, Herr Sattler, thank you."

"Don't mention it. Please, come with me." As he walked out from behind the desk, the Scottish couple came in from the breakfast room and Sattler smiled and said, "Good morning, Mr. and Mrs. Saunders. Have you met our English guest, Mr. Hirst?"

Mr. Saunders looked like he'd never set eyes on Conrad in his life, but his wife looked staggered. She gave him a pinched smile and said, "I think we met briefly in the breakfast room."

"Yes," said Conrad. "I do apologize if I came across as abrupt. I assumed you were German, and I really don't speak any at all."

"Nor do I," said Mr. Saunders, as if expressing a disdain for some unsavory new fad.

"I see. Well, perhaps we'll see you later." Mrs. Saunders wasn't buying it and led her husband away with her opinion of Conrad unchanged or even lowered.

It made him realize once more that he wasn't convincing socially—he could check into hotels and travel first class, he could do it under false names when necessary, but he wasn't equipped for anything more complex. It was like he'd learned the essentials of a language from a phrase book, but was unable to venture any further with it.

Sattler smiled as he watched the others walk away and then said, "A charming man and woman, Mr. and Mrs. Saunders. They come for one week every year since fifteen years."

Conrad looked at him and said, "Surely you haven't been here that long?"

"Naturally. I grew up here. I was a boy when Mr. and Mrs. Saunders came first." He smiled, and Conrad imagined it the smile of a man who was rooted in a place, no desire to escape, content with the cocoon of familiarity that surrounded every single one of his daily actions.

And as much as he could never have lived like that himself, even if his parents had still been alive and if the family home had still been there for him, he couldn't help but envy Sattler. Of course, orderly and attractive surfaces could conceal the shabbiest of lives, but Sattler's enthusiastic grin looked genuine enough as he said, "Now, let's get you some skis. A beautiful day is waiting for you."

Conrad followed Sattler, wondering what he'd think if he knew the truth, that Conrad not only knew all about their controversial local resident, but that he also killed for him. And he wondered what Sattler would think if he knew these skis would help Conrad plan that same person's murder.

Not that he really thought of it as a murder. He'd murdered Klemperer, he accepted that, just as he'd murdered the dozens of men and three women before him who'd had the misfortune of getting in the way of Eberhardt's business.

Whatever face Eberhardt showed the world, whatever social position he tried to cultivate, he was a man of violence, just as Conrad was. Neither of them could claim any moral protection if that violence rebounded upon them— their objections would be as hollow as a thief's outrage at being burgled.

Killing Eberhardt would not be murder, just as killing Frank the previous night hadn't been. They'd been in business together, them and Freddie and Fabio Gaddi, that was all, a partnership of sorts, and this was Conrad's way of dissolving that partnership. He even doubted that any of them would have objected to his method; they'd have objected only to the fact that he had made the first move.

3

CONRAD had spent a whole day cross-country skiing as a teen-ager and hated it. His father had nagged him into it in typical fashion—it was only one day away from the slopes, it would be another string to his bow, helpful for his army career.

He was grateful for that day now. The exercise was test-ing his fitness, but just as Sattler had predicted, the rudiments of the technique had come back to him quickly enough. And it *was* beautiful out there, so newly made, so clean and light, and possessed of intangible memories.

It made him realize, too, that for all he'd experienced, his feelings might not be so far removed from those of other people. By thirty-two, perhaps everyone felt a little jaded. Perhaps spring mornings and familiar landscapes and sights filled everyone of a certain age with a longing for something out of reach, partial recollections of feelings that wouldn't quite coalesce into the same joy or love or excitement.

And like all those others, he had to accept that sorrow and regret were part of the payoff for having memories to call upon. Perhaps the secret was to take the moment for what it was and not compare it to a sun-filtered past. This was the moment, him and this transient landscape, complementing each other perfectly.

Conrad was taking an indirect route toward the village, cutting between clumps of pines that were already glistening with melting snow, stopping regularly to get his breath back and to map a way forward that avoided any steep climbs.

He still couldn't help but think back to that day, and to the holiday itself, the last skiing holiday his family had taken together. He'd wanted to ask his father that morning why he was so certain Conrad would join the army, but he'd stopped himself, knowing he'd inevitably follow a family tradition that was, as far as he knew, only two generations old.

And if it hadn't been for the car crash, if he hadn't been orphaned at the woefully unsympathetic age of twenty, maybe that's where he would have been even now. The thought hung there for a moment, then jarred disconcertingly, because as clear as it had been in his mind, he'd remembered incorrectly.

It hadn't been the car crash—he'd already left the officer training corps at the end of his first year at college, and had simply never told them. An argument postponed for six months and then rendered unnecessary by something as mundane as a tire blowing out.

The mistake threw his concentration so much that he stumbled for the first time and sank into the snow as he landed. He struggled quickly to his feet, alarmed, desperate to snap out of it. He wiped some of the snow from his clothes, then stood for a few seconds, trying to work out how he could have falsely remembered something so fundamental.

He forced himself to go through the order in his head—

he'd dropped out of the OTC at the end of the summer term, first year; he'd informed the army because of the scholarship that would have to be returned; he'd meant to tell his parents that summer in France but the holiday had seemed too perfect to spoil; there had been too many people around at Christmas; the police had come to his room in January. He remembered it all and was relieved.

Any other time, the thought of forgetting something like this wouldn't have bothered him, but it did now. It was because of what Frank had said, he knew it, but he was disturbed by the thought of his memory tricking him like that, by anything that suggested he wasn't at least in control of his own mind, that other things might equally have slipped away from him.

He started to feel cold standing there and skied on, plagued by the doubts of the previous night. This was why it was important to write the letters, because he'd drifted away from himself, and talking to Anneke, dreaming of talking to Anneke, was the only way he could imagine pinning it all back down.

He rounded the next stand of trees and stopped again to look down on the small chapel with its onion-domed tower and the thinly spread hamlet of snow-laden roofs. The main part of the chapel seemed to be on the first floor, with covered wooden steps running up the front from both left and right, meeting in the middle, the appearance of a little Calvary that worshippers had to climb to gain access.

He checked his watch, then took out his binoculars and looked as a couple of people arrived on foot for the service. The couple waved, and he turned and gained focus on another well-wrapped woman coming from the other direction.

Conrad continued to turn his head slowly, following the path of the road, hoping to catch the arrival of Eberhardt's car. He wasn't even sure which way it was to the estate, but as he scanned the landscape he heard a car door, the sound carrying crisply, and he turned back quickly to see a black Mercedes sitting outside the chapel.

One suited man was already out of the car—the door he'd heard closing. He looked theatrically up and down the street like a presidential bodyguard, then opened the passenger door. Another man got out, and he knew it had to be him. Conrad couldn't see him clearly from up there, but he could see that Eberhardt had grayed considerably over these last nine years and that satisfied him somehow, as if it represented more than the natural progression of time.

Eberhardt walked up the covered wooden steps to the chapel, but the bodyguard stayed at the car and a few moments later the driver stepped out and joined him. At first he thought they were smoking, but as one of them moved he could see they had a flask of something hot and two mugs.

He let the binoculars go and looked at the landscape. If he stayed at the same level instead of descending into the bowl of the village, there was an uneven growth of trees which looked like it might give him a good line. He made for it, stopping every fifty yards or so to look at the changing perspective of the village, making sure he'd read the landscape correctly.

It took him around half an hour to get there, but it was a good spot, maybe a little far for a novice sniper, but with a clear shot of the chapel and Eberhardt's waiting car. His two men had given up on the cold now and were sitting back inside.

He stared through his binoculars, imagining they were a rifle sight, tracing Eberhardt's likely progress down the covered steps where he'd be surrounded by other worshippers. There was only a stretch of about ten paces between the steps and the car, where once again he'd be part of a group. Once he got to the car, though, there would be a few seconds with a clear exposure of his head and only trees behind if Conrad overcompensated for bullet drop. If he missed, there was a good chance they wouldn't even know he'd made an attempt, clearing him for another week.

Conrad made a mental marker of where the trees stood in relation to the village, imagining the entire scene without snow because it was forecast to be gone within the week, hard as that was to believe in the middle of it all. He worked his way carefully down toward the village, seeing if there was anywhere closer that provided the same level of access and cover.

Once he was down at the level of the chapel he took off the skis and stood them in the snow next to a store shed. He walked into the road and strolled away from the chapel, studying the buildings like a tourist would have done, glancing up to place his stand of trees from different positions.

He was certain he'd found the right spot—the gun would have to make up for any shortfalls in his ability from that distance. And like Frank had said, Conrad would have to accept the possibility of incidental casualties. The next priority was planning an escape route, but he wanted to see them come out of church first.

He noticed the bodyguard and the driver were out of the car again, so he headed casually in their direction. They weren't drinking this time but stamping their feet and chatting quietly, an air of expectancy about them. Sure enough, as Conrad approached, a couple of kids came running noisily down the steps, then some of the other parishioners.

He spotted the figure of Eberhardt among them and hurried his pace. He was confident Eberhardt wouldn't recognize him, not with a ski hat and sunglasses, particularly after nine years. And Conrad wanted to see how many people were around him as he got close to his car. To some extent, he just wanted to see Eberhardt up close one more time, to see what was in the face of the man he'd killed so many people for.

Eberhardt was near the bottom of the wooden steps, his back to Conrad, but then someone farther up the steps called out, "Herr Eberhardt." He turned, smiling as he saw the middle-aged woman, and said something back to her.

Conrad stopped walking and Eberhardt looked over at him, studying him with a cold eye, maybe assessing the threat. Conrad stared back, unable to help himself, his mind reeling back to his meeting with Eberhardt nine years before and to the events that had led up to it.

A job had gone wrong in Stuttgart, a simple job. Conrad had misunderstood an instruction from Schmidt and killed a man, in a moment, just a confused moment. Schmidt had predicted big trouble after that one, but a couple of nights later, Frank had brought Eberhardt to Conrad's room in Die Alpenrose.

Even now, standing here in the cold, it relaxed him to remember that room, the calm it had given him in those first weeks. He'd sit there night after night, looking up at the lonely light of the cable car station on the mountain, finding peace in the sight of it.

That's how they'd found him that evening. The three of

them had sat in the rustic prettiness of his room, and Eberhardt had talked to him about killing and secrecy, telling him he could use a man like him, but only if his discretion could be relied upon completely.

Conrad remembered it all. He couldn't remember how he'd felt, if he'd felt anything, but he remembered the details. And he remembered Eberhardt, barely a trace of an accent in his voice, his brown hair flecked with gray, the look of a man who didn't like to make himself comfortable.

He thought of it now, and in a strange way, it was a relief to have at least a sense of what Frank had been hinting at the previous night. Here he was, standing in the cold, staring at the puzzled face of Julius Eberhardt—he was a crime boss, that was for sure, but this wasn't the man he'd met nine years before. This was not his Eberhardt.

Frank had lied to Conrad, about everything. Those had been his dying words, but they didn't come close to the enormity of this revelation. Those early jobs with Schmidt had been for Eberhardt. He could be certain of it, because Schmidt hadn't been smart enough to be part of a lie that big, and because he'd lived and breathed Eberhardt like a vassal to a king.

But nine years ago in Mittenwald Frank had told Conrad the biggest lie of all, probably singling him out specifically because he wouldn't question the jobs he was given or the motives for them. Everything Conrad had done since, every aspect of his life over those years, had been a fabrication, a cover story for a truth he couldn't even begin to speculate upon.

He realized quickly that Frank had also worked for Eberhardt. And briefly, Conrad imagined a scenario in which the boss had simply sent someone in his place to Mittenwald,

31

but Conrad couldn't see why Eberhardt would have done that or how it would have served him.

The only rational explanation was the most troubling. Frank had served two masters, the other so dangerous or morally repugnant that he thought even Conrad, broken and pliable as he was, might have refused to kill for him.

Eberhardt was talking animatedly to the woman now as the other parishioners dispersed. Conrad looked at the two bodyguards, the car, back up the hill at the stand of trees, trying to take in that none of it mattered anymore because this man almost certainly had no idea who he was, or that he'd ever worked for him.

He tried to rally his thoughts, telling himself this didn't mean the whole plan had to be abandoned. It was even possible that it would still only mean killing Gaddi and Fischer and one other, but nevertheless, he had to accept that this changed everything.

And the thing he had to take in most urgently was that it changed his immediate plans. Now it was Fabio Gaddi he had to visit first, because if anyone other than Frank had the information he needed it would be Gaddi, and for the first time in his life he desperately needed information. Perhaps he'd always needed it, and it had been his failure to seek it that had left him exposed like this, standing in the snow staring at a stranger.

For the best part of a decade, Conrad had been a professional killer, and now he'd probably set a whole new machine in motion by killing Frank, triggering alarms with persons unknown. The alarms in his own head were deafening, too—disorienting him and leaving him dazed, because it was no longer just a matter of killing four people. If he was going to stand any chance of getting out of this alive, he had to find out who he'd been killing people for.

Conrad Hirst

There's a fault line between fate and coincidence, and thinking too much about it would rob anyone of his sanity. Why were you standing in that exact spot in the marketplace? Why did I run the way I did that night—if I'd slowed my pace even a little, Lewis Jones would have been dead before I got there and maybe none of this would have happened.

A guy called Schmidt, no one you ever knew, told me to throw a drug dealer over a balcony. Schmidt had winked, that's what he'd told me afterward, that the idea was just to scare the guy. But I hadn't seen him wink and I was so dulled by that stage that throwing a man to his death meant nothing at all. As it happens, Schmidt was also dead within the year, though not by my hands.

But how can any of it make sense? I run obliviously to one man's rescue, I kill another because of a missed facial expression, you walk back to a market stall to collect the change you've forgotten—fractions either way and our lives would have been settled differently. Perhaps we'd have been living together now, married, children. Perhaps.

It was the Norwegian girl who told me you were dead. I can't remember her name. I'd never really paid her much attention until then. She was pretty enough, very quiet. I'd always had the impression she disapproved of me, because you were all in Yugoslavia to do good, part of the solution, whereas Jason and I were just adventurers, there for our own purposes only.

She answered the door that night, looking composed and normal at first, like everything was fine. It was only when she saw me that she broke down. The words sobbed out of her, and with each broken fact I became a little more mute. The others were all out, looking for Mette in the hospital, and she wanted me to go in. But I couldn't—I just held her for a minute and left.

I walked away at first, the truth of her words soaking through me, and before I knew it I was running, tears streaming down my cheeks. And as fast as I ran, I still couldn't burn off the excess of adrenaline, my hands shaking with it.

I wish I could describe exactly how I felt but I don't have the eloquence for it. I don't have the language to express how much I loved you, so how could I ever put into words what it felt like to lose you? I ran, that's all I can say.

I ran into a district that was strange to me and there in the ruins I managed to save Lewis Jones. I didn't even do much to save him, just caused enough of a blundering distraction to allow him to save himself. The man was as close to the edge as it was possible to be, an unpaid mercenary, hooked on painkillers, a metal plate in his head. But he'd been in the Welsh Guards and the SAS and in the year that followed he was the only certainty I had.

I realize none of this means a great deal to you, and it's

too late for me to tell the whole story, even if I could be relied upon to tell the truth, even if I ever knew the truth. All you need to know is that Jones gave me Frank Dillon's number in Mittenwald, that Frank Dillon introduced me to Eberhardt, and that Eberhardt was a lie.

I knew this seemed too easy, Anneke. I wanted to kill four people and be done with it. Well, I'm one down and things have already fallen apart. But I can't turn back. It's not even an option—I have nothing to turn back to. I'll kill Gaddi and Fischer and I'll find out from one of them who that fourth man was and I'll kill him.

I can imagine you asking me why I don't simply walk away and disappear, and maybe you'd be right. But how can I walk away when I don't know who I'm walking away from, or if they'll ever come after me? All through the years of my sickness, someone has been running my life, and if I'm to have any hope of recovering myself, I must know who it is.

I love you,
Conrad

4

THERE were soldiers in the background—American, he thought, even though they were only faintly visible, a huddle of regimented shadows. The emphasis of the photograph wasn't on them, but on a man in an overcoat and a homburg hat, and on the small delegation of men greeting him.

Also just in shot on the far right of the picture was another man walking away, and Conrad wondered if this was a photograph of that fabled staple of the Cold War, the prisoner swap. It certainly had the look of a border crossing or checkpoint, even though he could see no barrier.

It didn't look like Checkpoint Charlie, either. He'd seen that for real, only after it had become a tourist attraction. And even though this photograph dated back to the '50s or '60s when it would have looked different, he was certain it wasn't taken in Berlin. It had been taken at night, and beyond the small checkpoint building there was only darkness, no indication of other buildings lining a street, or of anything urban at all.

This was the world Klemperer had inhabited. Conrad

was looking through the disks he'd taken from the old man's house—a memoir in German and hundreds of photographs, some of documents on yellowed paper, most of people and scenes like the one on his computer screen now.

The Cold War was something that had always been in the background during his childhood, only for it to evaporate as he was becoming an adult. Of course, the disintegration of Yugoslavia, which had been both the high point and the undoing of Conrad's life, had been one of the consequences of that retreat from certainty.

He clicked onto the next picture, a portrait of a young Russian officer with a wide face and high cheekbones, medals on his chest, with an airbrushed quality to the photograph that made it look almost as if it had been rendered in pastels.

There were plenty of pictures like that, people he imagined being key players in the memoirs. But the interesting photographs were those that showed a dynamic, like the scene at the checkpoint, or a grainy picture of protesters in a depressingly imposing city street, another of two jaunty-looking men getting out of a black car, smiling at the photographer.

He studied that last picture more closely. One of the men was walking toward the camera, and even though he was wearing a double-breasted overcoat and a Russian-style fur hat, something about his face said he was an American, a healthy midwestern quality. The other man had been caught as he was about to close the driver's door, and he held his hat in his hand.

Just as his friend looked unquestionably American, so the second man looked German, the patrician Germanic looks that twenty years earlier would have appeared in similarly striking photographs, decked out in Wehrmacht or SS uniforms. And maybe this man had been just old enough to play a part in the war, but he still looked young in the picture, full of energy and optimism.

Perhaps when the picture was taken, he'd had every reason to be optimistic, a charmed life ahead of him. Even so, it made Conrad sad in some imprecise way because the young man was Hans Klemperer himself, and a few weeks earlier, Conrad had exchanged a few pleasantries with him before hanging him from an exposed beam in his own bedroom.

There was no reason for him to sympathize with a man who'd lived to seventy-six, a man whose life had been full, and who, judging from this photograph and all the others that had been intended to illustrate his memoirs, had little to regret when set against the bleak emptiness of Conrad's life.

But then, photographs captured moments, not lives. His own brief flirtation with becoming a photographer seemed as distant as these pictures now, only none of his had survived as far as he knew. He thought of some of the pictures he'd taken, in Egypt and the Far East, then in Yugoslavia, and he could think of only one that told the truth.

Likewise, if Conrad had kept his camera with him through the fighting, maybe he'd have captured himself and others in their company—stray smiles, shared bottles, creating a false impression of camaraderie, of life being lived on the edge. Those photographs would have been lies, so it was possible that Klemperer's were, too. Perhaps the only pertinent truth was that both of them, separated by nearly fifty years, had ended up alone.

Of course, there was one aspect of Klemperer's life Conrad didn't intend to share. Apparently, the old man had twice managed to avoid assassination over the years, even encouraging one of his would-be killers to defect in the process. But Klemperer had made too many contacts and learned too many secrets, so it seemed inevitable in retrospect that his luck would run out eventually.

Conrad thought of the old man's body hanging limply from the beam and it spurred him on, because he didn't want to live another forty years always waiting for the fatal knock on the door. He took the disk out and put one of the others back in, the one that contained the memoirs. He did a word search on "Eberhardt," then removed the disk when it came up blank. He'd wanted to be sure, but Klemperer had been telling the truth when he'd told him the name meant nothing to him.

Conrad laughed, his thoughts catching up as he reminded himself that Eberhardt meant nothing to him, either. Somewhere in those memoirs he would quite possibly find the name of the man who'd masqueraded as Eberhardt, who'd actually been his boss for nine years, the man who'd ordered Klemperer's death to prevent this book ever being published.

He imagined that name would also be found somewhere in the disks he'd taken from Frank, but they were all encrypted. For the time being, he had no choice but to act blind and follow the only leads he had, Gaddi and Fischer.

But he couldn't shake the intriguing prospect that these two worlds, these two sets of disks taken from dead men, were somehow intertwined. At some point, someone in the world he'd inhabited had sanctioned the death of a former spy and Cold War player.

He got up and walked through to the sitting room, looking out the window at the street some way below, then at the building opposite. It was easy now to imagine a surveillance team over there on the top floor, taking his picture, adding it to a portfolio that wouldn't have looked out of place on Klemperer's disks.

As problematic as it would have been, as much as it would have thrown his current plans even further into confusion, it was a seductive fantasy. But he knew the reality would be more prosaic. If Frank had kept the truth from him, his real employer had undoubtedly been someone infinitely more unpalatable than the real Eberhardt.

Or possibly the truth that Frank had concealed was that he'd had no fixed employer at all, that Frank had simply been contracting out his services to anyone who had the money to pay for them. Whatever structure had shored up his life, there was no glamor to be retrieved from these nine years.

He had to be grateful for that, because as much of a setback as it had been in Birkenstein, the one thing that remained unchanged was the phantom existence he'd lived. He knew how few people he'd dealt with in the course of his work. He was no longer sure of all the names, but he had no reason to believe he'd been wrong in his calculations and every reason to believe there were still only three more bridges to burn.

He'd deposit all of the disks at the bank before he left for Milan. They were of no value to him, possibly of no value to anyone, but after the Eberhardt surprise, it was better to play everything more cautiously, and that meant leaving nothing in the apartment that could connect him to any of these people.

After that, he just had to hope he could get Gaddi to tell

him the name of the fourth man, the other Eberhardt who was increasingly becoming the focus of his thoughts. He'd still kill Gaddi and Fischer because the fundamentals hadn't changed and he'd be exposed as long as any of them lived, but he knew instinctively that the fourth man was the key to getting out permanently and safely.

He didn't feel he had any right to seek revenge, nor did he feel he could blame anyone but himself for the things he'd done. He wasn't the wronged party in this. For all he knew, there were no wronged parties—perhaps even his victims, perhaps even Klemperer, had blackened personal histories of their own.

But if atonement was something he had to go through to fix himself, part of the process was finding that other Eberhardt, finding out who he was and why he'd employed him. Part of it was killing him. And even as he thought like this, he knew it summed up everything that was wrong with his life, that the only way he could see of atoning for all his killing was to kill again.

He knew it didn't make sense. He knew it was wrong, but as much as he'd never wanted to kill anyone, as neutral a killer as he'd been, he actually *wanted* to kill the man who'd employed him all those years ago in a hotel room in Mittenwald.

He knew nothing about him, not even his name. He knew so little that he couldn't understand the strength of his own feelings, but nevertheless, he wanted to kill him.

5

THE paranoia started to kick in on the way to the station. He turned and glanced out the back window of the taxi, then casually turned sideways in his seat. He was convinced that a black Jeep sitting a few vehicles back had been parked up near the bank.

At a conscious level, he could see how ridiculous it was and knew that anyone setting out to tail him would have chosen a slightly less conspicuous vehicle. He even knew the whole notion of him being tailed was ridiculous. He'd spent too much time looking at Klemperer's disks the night before, and now a part of his brain was clinging stubbornly to the Cold War scenario of being tailed, of being under surveillance. He'd be searching his apartment for bugs next.

Reason didn't help though, and he was equally touchy as he waited on the platform, reading too much into the casual glances of strangers, studying their luggage. They were just business people for the most part, but he was still relieved when the train came and he was able to settle into the more containable world of the first-class carriage.

He sat at an empty table, but before the train left an over-weight guy in his fifties came and sat opposite him, wearing a pale gray suit and a mustard scarf that he left on even after removing his coat. He gave Conrad a vaguely disdainful look, perhaps because Conrad was wearing casual clothes; the guy probably wondered what he was doing in first class with all the other business travelers.

The guy was bursting at the seams and breathing hard with every movement. He took out a laptop, struggled to arrange his briefcase on the seat next to him, documents on the table next to the computer. Conrad's ticket was on the table, and he caught the guy glancing at it.

For a couple of hours, Conrad stared out the window or closed his eyes and listened to the guy's labored breathing and heavy-handed keyboard skills, then watched him rush to get things together at Strasbourg. It was lunchtime, so Conrad put his bag on his seat, took his rucksack, and walked through to the dining car.

By the time he got back, there was a woman in his seat, probably in her mid-twenties, though she could have passed for younger, with blond, bobbed hair and a rosy-cheeked complexion. Her girl-next-door looks were slightly at odds with her clothes, which were at the high-fashion end of smart casual—a dark mix of bohemian and gothic.

Conrad looked down at his bag, which had been moved to the opposite seat. She looked up from the paperback she was reading and said, "I'm sorry, is that your bag? I hope you don't mind, but I have to sit facing the engine."

She was American, a friendly enthusiasm in her voice that added to the illusion of youth, making her sound like a college student. Conrad moved his bag and sat down. The book she was reading was in French.

"I don't mind. How did you know I spoke English?"

She looked a little pleased with herself and said, "I didn't. I speak French and German but, frankly, working in Strasbourg, I find English is always a good opening play." She put her hand out and said, "Alice Benning."

It seemed a little premature for introductions, but her friendliness was infectious enough that he shook her hand and said, "Conrad Hirst."

"From and to?" He looked confused and she laughed. "Formalities are always so boring. I'm asking where you're coming from and going to. I mean on this train as opposed to life in general."

"I see," he said, talking despite himself. For all his earlier paranoia, there was something so natural about her, it was hard to resist the recklessness of a conversation. "I'm out of Luxembourg, going to Milan."

"Oh, me too! Say, have you been there before—you might know where my hotel is." She rummaged in her bag and pulled out a piece of paper, reading from it in a decent Italian accent. "Excelsior Hotel Gallia, Piazza Duca D'Aosta."

He smiled and said, "That's where I'm staying." And it had to be a coincidence or she wouldn't have mentioned it so soon.

"Amazing! Maybe we could share a cab?"

"I don't think so." She looked a little thrown, but he smiled and said, "It's really right around the corner from the station. We could walk."

"Well, aren't you a tease, Conrad Hirst!" She'd been holding her book open but put the bookmark in now and placed it on the table, clearly thinking he was worth talking to. He wasn't so sure and was wondering if this would prove a long five hours. "So what's your line of business?"

"I'm a security consultant, dealing with computer systems." She pretended to look impressed. "I know, it's really boring, but I get paid a lot for very little work." That much was true, at least. "And what about you, Alice?"

"I'm a journalist. I work on *The Economist.*"

He nodded and was enjoying her easygoing presence, but the watchful voice in his head was telling him now that she'd just made her first mistake. He hadn't been consciously thinking that she might not be what she seemed, because he'd never needed to think like that before Eberhardt and was still new to it, but now the dam had broken and nothing was right about her.

She could have been a journalist on any paper and it wouldn't have aroused his suspicions, but she'd claimed to work for the one magazine which famously didn't use bylines, making it impossible to run a check on her. And something about the way she was dressed didn't fit either, not with the job, not with her. Add to that the fact that she'd chosen his seat, that she was staying in his hotel, and he couldn't help but become cautious.

"Do you know anyone in the London office?"

"I've met some of them but I couldn't say I know any of them. I've only been in the job three months."

"So you don't know Frank Dillon?"

He studied her eyes, but they gave nothing away and she sounded genuine as she said, "Are you sure he works for *The Economist*? The name really doesn't ring a bell at all."

Conrad smiled, the first increment of reassurance in place, and said, "You know, I'm not sure, and I don't even know why I mentioned him. It might have been Reuters now that I think of it, and I haven't seen the guy in five years anyway."

She laughed in a good-natured way, no indication that she thought she was being tested, and said, "So what's it like living in Luxembourg? Do you have family there?"

"It's okay, and no, I don't." He guessed she'd want a little more than that, so he added, "My parents are in England, no brothers or sisters."

"Single?"

Why had no one engaged him in conversation like this before? Was it just another coincidence to add to the many? Or was it that he'd already changed, that over the last two weeks he'd become more approachable? It seemed unlikely somehow that he could have begun to find himself again so quickly.

"Single," he said, wondering as he answered if she'd be shocked at exactly how single he was, how isolated his life had been. "What about you?"

"I'm single, too. Parents and a sister are in Pennsylvania, my brother's in New York. And Strasbourg is okay also." She smiled to herself. "I have to tell you, my dad was terrified of me coming over here. He was scared the plane would crash, he's checking online to see how safe it is living in Strasbourg, lecturing me on how I had to be careful with European men. You'd think I was still eighteen or something."

"I have to say you don't look much older."

She didn't look flattered, but gave a reluctantly acknowledging nod and said, "I'm thirty, as it happens. I know I look a lot younger and I probably should be grateful for that, but it's hard to get taken seriously sometimes."

Maybe that was why her clothes looked odd. She'd have looked natural in the clothes of a student, but anything more stylized was always going to look too old for her—office clothes probably would have looked stranger still.

"Maybe you should drink more and sleep less—that'll do the trick."

She laughed, and he realized this was the first time in years that he'd met a stranger and made them laugh. He wasn't transformed yet, he couldn't be, but it did feel like he'd taken one more step on the road to normality that had opened up seductively in Chur a couple of weeks ago.

"So how come you're single?"

"How come you are?"

She pretended to object, saying, "Er, excuse me, but I just moved here three months ago. You've been living in Luxembourg how long?"

"Nine years. So you weren't single before you came here?"

"I broke up with a boyfriend six months ago. That was part of the reason I took the job, and don't think I haven't noticed that you haven't answered the question."

"Nothing to answer. Why is anyone ever single?"

"True," she said, looking briefly wistful, as if she wouldn't need much more of an excuse to talk all day about relationships.

He wanted to get off the subject, urgently, so he pointed at her book and said, "You read French?"

She looked at the book, too, as if reminding herself of its existence. "I can read French, and German if pushed, but I don't usually. I just didn't have anything else to read. I'm such a bookworm."

"Have you read anything by Jason Fleming?"

"Of course!" She looked excited by the mention of the name. "I love his books. Is that what you read?"

He shook his head, saying, "I'm not much of a reader. I should I suppose, but . . . I used to know him, that's all."

"Get out of here!" She looked as surprised as if he'd said he knew a famous actor or pop star, and it seemed strange to Conrad that anyone could be that impressed by the mention of a writer. "How? Were you at college together or something?"

"No. We met traveling on the backpacker trail, years ago, Egypt, Thailand, and we both went to Yugoslavia together, during the war out there."

Eyes wide in disbelief, she said, "You *chose* to go to a war zone? Why would you do that?"

"It sounds crazy but a lot of people were doing it. I think people saw it as our generation's Spanish Civil War, which it wasn't, obviously."

"In some ways it was better." He looked questioningly. "I see what you're getting at, that there wasn't exactly a right side and a wrong side in Yugoslavia, but to the extent that there *was* a right side, I think it won. In Spain the wrong side won."

Conrad nodded and said, "If I'm honest, what I really meant is that they went for principle, whereas we went for the kick. That's how Jason sold it to me, that we'd be the new Hemingway and Capa, but it was the idea of being like them that appealed, nothing to do with what they stood for."

She'd been almost bizarrely outgoing from the second he'd sat down and had shown a generalized interest in what he had to say, but he could see now that she was really intrigued by the mention of Yugoslavia. He liked that he was talking about it, too, because he'd never talked to anyone about that time, not even the period before the shells had fallen on the marketplace.

"Oh, I think Hemingway and Capa were just as in love with the idea of being Hemingway and Capa. I'm guessing that's who you were—Capa?"

He laughed a little. "It's who Jason wanted me to be. I just wanted to be a photographer."

"So what happened? Why the move into computer security?"

"I lost interest. And it looks like Jason didn't."

She was struck by a thought and said, "You know, there's a character in one of his books, I can't remember the title, but he's a photographer . . ."

"Yeah, I believe so."

She looked excited by the prospect as she said, "It's not based on you, surely?"

"I don't know. I doubt it somehow."

She seemed disappointed and said, "You're not in touch anymore?"

"No. We kind of got separated by the war. It's so recent, it's hard to believe this was before everyone had mobile phones and e-mail addresses; we just had no way of tracking each other down."

"You could track him down now." She gave it a little thought herself and added, "Still, I guess some friendships belong in a certain period of your life. It's like people you meet on vacation."

"Or on trains?"

She smiled slyly and said, "Well, if we only have a few hours, I have a whole lot of questions about Yugoslavia and enough stories about me to last you a lifetime."

The time went by easily enough. Alice was good company, and with them being around the same age, a lot of their conversation revolved around the differences between growing up in America and England, college life and so on, music and television, common cultural reference points.

He was able to talk about his childhood without ever mentioning that it had ended with the death of his parents, and college without mentioning that he'd left halfway through, or that he'd met Jason in Egypt where he was trying to see how much of his inheritance he could burn through on the backpacker trail. He talked about Yugoslavia, too, or at least, the first part of it.

The trouble was, even as he talked to Alice and warmed to her, even as he imagined her in more casual clothes and then not in clothes at all, he still had surges of doubt. He'd been killing people for someone unknown, Frank had lied to him, Frank had been an American, here was an American spontaneously striking up a conversation with him, sharing life stories, someone his age who just happened to sit in his seat.

There was something else, too. She was expansive about her childhood, her family, college, what she thought of different places in Europe, so expansive that he didn't notice at first that there was a huge gap. There seemed to be no stories between college and now, nothing of her years in journalism.

Maybe most people didn't have stories to tell about their twenties, but he was aware that his life story contained a similar gap, and knowing what filled it made him acutely aware that Alice Benning could be anyone, could work for anyone. And maybe it wasn't so paranoid to think she could have been planted on the train, primed to ask all the right questions.

The only weakness in Conrad's thinking was that he had nothing to offer. If the people who'd been employing him were onto the fact that he'd killed Frank and was making a break for it, the only thing they could possibly want from him was his death.

He could do nothing other than play it cautiously, treating her at face value, looking out for trip wires in the conversation. If he wasn't paranoid and Alice did have something else in mind, he guessed he'd only have to wait till Milan to find out what it was.

If she wanted information from him, she was in for a disappointment. Equally, if she was intending to lead him to his death, she'd quite possibly underestimated how determined he was, and how ruthless. He liked her and, hard as it was to believe, he hoped for her sake that she simply enjoyed his company.

It was raining in Milan, a fine drizzle that could hardly be felt but showed up under the streetlights like a gauze veil. Conrad pointed the way, and as they walked he said, "I read in a book once—"

She interrupted him, a light-hearted tease as she said, "Oh, so you have read a book?"

"One or two," he said, laughing off the interjection. It felt as if he'd known her much longer than five hours. "Anyway, I think it's the Turks, but they call this 'idiots' rain.'"

"I think I've read that book," she said. "People can't see it, so they make false assumptions about how bad it is."

He looked at her, getting the feeling she was talking about anything but the rain. She smiled back at him, her expression disarming, so he said, "Something like that."

"Do you have plans for dinner?"

He was tempted, despite the alarm bells which had sounded intermittently since he'd found her sitting in his seat, but without giving himself time to think about it, he said, "I have a meeting planned. Some other time maybe."

"I didn't say I was offering, I was just curious." She laughed, but then said, "It must be an important job for you to hit the ground running like this."

Playing her at her own game, he said, "Who said it was business?"

"Touché," she said, as if they'd been sparring like this for years.

As they walked into the hotel she stopped and looked around, saying, "Oh, isn't this wonderful. I love Art Deco."

He looked around like he'd never seen it before, even though this was the third time he'd stayed here. He had no idea whether it was Art Deco but he supposed it was imposing enough, plenty of mahogany and marble. Maybe a decade earlier he'd have been spotting details, wielding his camera here and there—now it was just another space he was passing through, and it took someone like Alice Benning to tell him it was beautiful.

One of the receptionists was busy checking in another guest, so they walked to the other clerk and Conrad gestured for her to go first.

"Hello. Alice Benning, checking in."

The receptionist looked at the computer and then back at the two of them, a puzzled expression as he said, "You are together?"

She laughed and said, "No, we met on the train." The other receptionist was free, so Conrad walked around Alice and checked in with him.

Still playing safe, he said, "I'm expecting a guest. Has anyone called for me?" The receptionist checked and found nothing. Alice acted as if she hadn't even heard him, but he was certain she had and, no matter who she was, it was better that she thought his meeting would be here in the hotel.

"Maybe I'll see you in the bar," she said hopefully as she was shown up to her room.

"Maybe," he said. "Good meeting you, anyway."

"You too, Conrad."

He watched as she walked away to the elevator, then turned to his receptionist, who was also looking on approvingly. He smiled, offering Conrad a knowing look. Conrad ignored it, handing him a tip instead, and said, "Have my bag taken to my room. I have to go out."

He picked up a cab and handed the driver Gaddi's address. He'd posted things to him in the past but had never actually been there, not even on his two previous visits to Milan, and he had little idea what to expect.

As it was, Gaddi lived in an upmarket apartment building. Conrad rang the bell a couple of times, then tried the bell for the porter. He'd been standing at the door a couple of minutes when a dark-haired guy of about forty approached along the street, wearing a raincoat, carrying a briefcase and an umbrella.

The guy stopped to put his umbrella down and shake off the rain. He was wearing glasses and they were spotted with rain, too. He smiled at Conrad, looking vaguely expectant.

Conrad pointed inside and said, "Porter?"

"You're English?" Conrad nodded and the guy looked at his watch. "No, it's too late for the porter. You're looking for someone?"

"Fabio Gaddi."

"Ah, Signor Gaddi." He frowned, opening the door as he said, "I think he's gone. Come inside, we'll ask his neighbor."

"Thank you." Conrad stepped into the lobby behind him and said, "You think he's gone? You mean he's away?"

As the stranger led the way to the elevator, he said, "He's left. My wife told me yesterday, she saw him. He said he had to move away, for work."

He took Conrad up to the fourth floor, cleaning his glasses with a silk handkerchief as the elevator ascended. It clearly wasn't his own floor, and he checked the nameplates before finding the right door and knocking. An elderly man answered, moneyed, well groomed and well dressed with a waistcoat, checked shirt, and cravat.

They exchanged greetings and then the stranger asked the old man about Gaddi. The response was long-winded, supported by lots of to-and-fro hand movements, the old man becoming exasperated recounting it.

Finally, the stranger pointed at the door opposite and said, "That is Signor Gaddi's apartment, but he says it's quite empty. They have been coming and going all day long. He complained to them about the noise."

The old man added something else but it didn't seem to add anything new and remained untranslated.

Conrad said, "Does he mean moving men?"

"Yes," said the stranger, but sought confirmation from the old man, who shook his head and pointed at Conrad as he launched into another tirade. The stranger looked perplexed as he said, "He says they were dressed like moving men but they weren't Italian. He says they were English or American, like you."

Conrad was having trouble assessing what this meant, and his voice was on autopilot as he said, "Just one more question. Could you ask him if Signor Gaddi had mentioned that he might be moving?"

The answer was clear, the old man responding as if Gaddi had vanished into thin air. Conrad looked at the door, sensing the suddenly empty apartment beyond it, and realized that from his perspective, Gaddi had done exactly that.

"Thank you," he said to the helpful stranger. "And please tell the gentleman I'm sorry to have disturbed him. I'll see myself out."

Conrad was like a man sleepwalking, and only became conscious again as he stumbled back out into the cool mist of the rain. He knew immediately that he had to get off the street, that he couldn't afford to be caught in the open. Whatever the threat was, he had to assume not only that it had caught up with him, but that it was one step ahead.

He hadn't had time to think through what he'd just heard, let alone how it fit with everything else. At the moment, the events of the last few days were all as encrypted as the disks he'd taken from Frank's study, but whether he was paranoid or not, he understood instinctively that he had to start acting as if someone really was out to get him, at least until he knew what was going on.

He spotted a cab and flagged it down, and as he went back to the hotel he tried to piece together what the news about Gaddi meant. The most attractive but least likely theory was pure coincidence. It seemed like Gaddi had moved in a hurry, and he could only imagine it being in response to Frank's death.

The moving men had been English or American, which suggested Gaddi had no more worked for Eberhardt than Conrad had. Or alternatively, it meant that Gaddi had served two masters, just as Frank had, with Eberhardt unwittingly acting as little more than cover for whatever the real business was.

The best he could hope for was that they didn't know he'd killed Frank, that he wasn't even on their radar. That brought him back to Alice Benning. It was a shame and he'd fought against it, but he had to treat her as someone who meant him harm. Any other explanation was just too much of a stretch from reality, certainly his reality.

What was more, if Alice was part of it, they had his movements pretty well figured, too. That was something else he'd have to combat, not least because it meant he was up against someone well organized, maybe a government agency of some kind. And just twenty-four hours on, that no longer seemed a ludicrous idea at all.

He asked the receptionist to prepare his bill and call him a taxi for the airport, then walked toward the stairs. He spotted her far too late. She was sitting in one of the armchairs in the small lounge area next to the stairs, waving at him, smiling as she waited for him to notice.

"Goodness, you look serious."

He tried a smile and said, "Miles away, sorry."

"Don't be. Time for a drink?"

He leaned on the back of the chair opposite and said, "I have to make a couple of phone calls." He looked at his watch. "Will you still be around in an hour?"

She looked noncommittal. "I might be. You know, I won't wait forever, Conrad. It's only a drink."

He smiled and walked up the stairs. Even if she was genuine, he was beginning to think she was a little too pushy, a hint of desperation about her. After all, he doubted he was that much of a catch, and if she was just being friendly, then maybe her father had been right to worry about her because she really was an innocent.

The lights were turned low in Conrad's room, curtains drawn, bed turned down. He called and asked for a porter, and as he waited, he stood soaking up the hush of the room, the soft focus efforts of the staff to ensure him a restful evening, all in vain.

The porter tried hard not to betray his surprise at the small bag he was being asked to carry, but Conrad gave him a decent tip and asked him to carry it down to the taxi. He waited a minute or so, then followed.

Alice was no longer sitting near the stairs, but he took no chances, stopping at the reception desk long enough only to tell them to charge it to his card. The receptionist wanted him to check the bill and sign it, but he was out the doors and on his way to the airport with those polite protestations still hanging in the air.

He didn't know how amateurish his thinking was and had no way of quantifying the professionalism of the people he imagined himself being up against. Either way, he guessed they'd get some information out of the hotel staff, even if it was only that he'd left in a taxi for the airport.

If they were smart, they'd realize it was a bluff, that he couldn't fly with hardware and wouldn't fly without it. He rented a car at the airport, using a false passport and card, but again, given that every identity had been obtained for him by Gaddi, he didn't expect it to throw off the scent for long. He would still have a brief advantage over them, a window of freedom in which they'd be reduced to guessing his likely movements, and maybe it would take them a while to work out that there was only one place he was likely to go.

He drove through the night to Zurich, abandoned the car, and picked up an early train to St. Margrethen, finding a connection from there to take him around the lake to Lindau.

It was still before ten when he reached the hotel, the lobby busy with people checking out. He approached the desk and asked for a room, not recognizing the young female receptionist. She was efficient, polite—a little too polite. Then Ulrich appeared and spotted him, immediately coming over and shooing the girl away.

"Mr. Hirst, what a wonderful surprise."

"Hello, Ulrich, it is unexpected, but good to see you." He liked Ulrich—helpful without being obsequious, friendly without being too familiar. He had a reassuring air about him, too, short gray hair, fastidious, like an ex-military man, indeterminately middle-aged. Even now, Conrad had no idea how old he was.

"Excellent, I see we have a room with a lake view ready for you now. Would you like a little breakfast perhaps, or some morning coffee?"

"I think so, maybe a cold plate, some coffee, juice. I'll take it in my room—I'm tired."

"Of course. And how many nights are you planning to stay?"

"One, maybe two."

Ulrich smiled and said, "You never stay long enough, Mr. Hirst. You need to relax more."

"I'm trying to arrange that," he said with a smile.

He took a shower once he got to his room, ate breakfast in his robe, then walked out onto his terrace. It was too cold to be out there like that and there was little to see, a heavy mist hanging on the lake, eating into the view of the waterfront. Even so, he stood for a few minutes, enjoying the illusion of being hidden, cut off from the world.

Ulrich was right, and maybe he would come back here when it was all taken care of, stay for a week or two. It was the only hotel he'd ever stayed in where people remembered him from one visit to the next. He thrived on not being remembered, a trait that was the foundation of this faltering bid for freedom, but he was still drawn to the sense of belonging that he felt here.

It saddened him, too, knowing that he wouldn't need to stay here again. Freddie Fischer was the only reason he'd ever come to Lindau, and their business relationship was about to end. Assuming he was still here—a big assumption under the circumstances—he'd go to his house this afternoon and kill him. If he'd disappeared . . . If Freddie had disappeared, Conrad wasn't entirely sure what he'd do. Killing was the only real skill he had.

Conrad Hirst

Dear Anneke,

I want to tell you about the first time I killed someone. It wasn't the night I saved Lewis Jones, the night of the day you died. I took a gun from a body that night and I aimed it at the men who'd captured Jones. But when it came to it, I fired over their heads. A crazy thing to do, but it proved sufficient, distracting them long enough for Jones to overpower and kill the four of them, like nothing I've ever seen since. I carried a gun from then on, but it was two months more before I killed anyone.

You'd be surprised how little killing goes on in a war. There's a lot of dying, there are bombs and shells, mines, there's wild gunfire that steals its small share of casualties. But there's not much one-on-one killing. Even now, I see reports of the massacres that took place and they seem at odds with what I knew. I try to imagine the men I knew doing those things and it just isn't possible. Of most of them, at least. Of Jones, or of myself, I'm not so sure.

After a week we became attached to a small militia unit.

Jones spoke some of the language and claimed to know someone in common with their commander. They let us tag along at first; and then we were just there, and they were used to us, to Jones with his occasional tics, always humming to himself, to me, contained and mute.

We saw some bad things in those first weeks. We saw action, too—chaotic, bordering on farcical. One man tripped a wire that blew a chunk out of his leg and we saw him bleed to death in a minute. Another was caught by a stray bullet in a nighttime skirmish, hit in the head, and didn't die until hours after they found him and a sickly dawn was breaking.

For the most part, it was much like the experience of the war you would have been familiar with, the war as I'd known it until then—intense silence full of ugly promise, intense noise that became a deafness of its own, hours and days of boredom, intervals of terror so overwhelming they only registered in the mind once they were over.

Two months after meeting Jones, we were involved in a skirmish and took a prisoner, a Serb boy of maybe seventeen. He was young but he was big, taller than everyone in our unit and solidly built, and he had the reddest hair I think I've ever seen.

He looked scared, more like a child who hadn't asked for this lumbering adult body or the uniform that came with it. The men seemed reasonably well disposed toward him and our commander was full of reassurances. Jones told me with some confidence that they wouldn't hurt him.

That was before they found the ears. The kid had a pouch on his belt with three left ears in it. It wasn't a particularly Serb thing, as far as I know. Some people in every war are prone to collecting trophies. Looking back, I can imagine the

kid being cajoled into it by some twisted superior. I also won-
der why he wasn't smart enough to get rid of them when he
was caught. Maybe he was just too scared to think straight.

The men became angry when they found the ears. One
smacked him hard around the head, but the kid didn't fall
down. Three or four of them started to beat him badly then.
The commander stayed out of it, sitting off to one side,
smoking a cigarette.

It was a measured beating, cruel, the blows deliberate,
and the kid didn't plead with them, he didn't shout out in
pain. He remained silent for at least the first ten minutes,
and then he started to cry and still tried to stifle his sobs.
He looked lonelier than anyone I've ever seen, a loneliness
that was terrible to witness, a boy wanting to be among his
own people, with his family and friends, the still-comforting
embrace of his mother.

I remember staring at the scene like I was watching it
on TV, powerless to intervene. And I couldn't understand
why the boy's sobbing seemed to enrage them more, why the
blows became fiercer. He was a child really, and they were
killing him, a slow painful death.

The thoughts were squalling in my head, and I couldn't
stand the sound—the boy's sobbing and the slaps and muf-
fled thumps—and I hated myself for sitting there letting it
happen. I hated myself for letting any of it happen. Every-
thing was swimming frantically in my head, all the misery,
everything from the moment of losing you to the poor boy
in front of me. And then something happened, and all those
thoughts started to swim in the same direction, seething,
forming an impenetrable wall.

I can't explain what I did. I don't remember getting up. It was as if I was woken by the gunshots and there I was standing over the boy, his head blown apart, and his tormentors looking at me with a mixture of fear and anger and astonishment. One of them said something fierce and looked like he might take it further, but I heard Jones stand up behind me and the guy changed his mind.

Then the commander said something and they dispersed. He came over, looked at the dead boy and spoke to Jones. He put his hand on my shoulder and said something to me, too. Finally, he looked at the boy again, expressing no compassion, almost looking relieved that the matter of what to do with him was out of his hands.

Jones told me afterward what the commander had said, that they wouldn't have killed him, that a beating didn't last forever. I asked him what he'd said to me, and it was meaningless enough at the time, but it came to sound like the words of an oracle in the years to come. "Now we won't be able to stop you."

And yet even as I write this now, I don't know when I became a killer. The crucial moment of that first death was lost in an instance of fractured consciousness. So were many of the crucial moments that followed. Then one day I killed someone as casually as I might have remembered to turn off a light on leaving a room. I still don't know how it happened, or where I lost the part of me that could have stopped it happening. Where did I go, Anneke? Where did I go?

Conrad

7

FREDDIE lived in a grand old merchant's townhouse on the island itself, not on one of the busiest streets, but still the kind of place that tourists strolled around during the day. It was a conspicuous spot for a specialized arms supplier, but he had good reasons for being there.

For one thing, Freddie had always believed there wasn't much point in making money from crime if he didn't use it to live in an attractive location. He liked the fact that the town was easily accessible from Switzerland, and more importantly, he liked the fact that it was a tourist haunt because there were very few real neighbors and everyone on the island was used to a steady stream of strangers coming and going.

Conrad wasn't quite so sure about the latter theory, reckoning that the tourists themselves were inevitably more observant than they would have been at home, and he was conscious of the half dozen people he could see now on the narrow, cobbled street where Freddie lived.

He stayed casual but he tried to be discreet when it came to knocking on the door, offering up no promise of local color. That was in vain—after just a few seconds the door was flung open by a young woman. She was full of expectation at first, then tried to conceal her disappointment.

She was slim, her long hair dark and wavy, a slight tan or a touch of olive in her skin, and despite the practical clothes—hiking boots, fitted jeans, a woolen sweater—she looked stunning, certainly attractive enough to draw the attention of anyone passing by.

"I'm sorry," she said, realizing he must have noticed how deflated she was. "I thought it was Freddie."

Her pronunciation was good, her accent unmistakably French, and for the second time in a couple of days, a young and attractive woman had spoken to him in English.

"How did you know I'm English?"

She looked bashful as she said, "I always talk English around Freddie. I don't speak German, he doesn't speak French."

It was a suspiciously convenient explanation, but she hadn't missed a beat in giving it. He wondered whether it might be best to back off, to come back some other time when Freddie was alone, but if he did that he ran the risk of losing whatever element of surprise was still his.

"Do you mind if I wait inside?"

She gave it some thought, then shrugged and stood back to let him in. There was a backpack—hers, he guessed—leaning against the wall in the hallway. And from where he stood, it didn't look like the house had been emptied, so it was still possible Freddie hadn't followed Fabio Gaddi into the ether.

"He's expecting you?"

Conrad turned and said, "No. No, he isn't." He glanced at the backpack. "And you? Does he know you're here?"

She squeezed her hand into the pocket of her jeans and pulled out a key, holding it up for him to see. "I called him yesterday to tell him I was coming. But I've been here an hour. I don't understand where he could be."

Conrad looked into the dining room and kitchen. Maybe the location and size of the house had prevented them emptying it the way they'd emptied Gaddi's apartment. Whatever the explanation, Conrad sensed that Freddie wouldn't be back at all, and was confident enough of the fact to blow his cover, saying, "I'm Conrad."

He held out his hand and she shook it, her own hand soft and tactile. "Delphine Racette."

"So, Delphine, you say you spoke to him yesterday, and he seemed fine? He didn't suggest it might be a problem you coming today?" She shook her head, baffled. "How do you know him?"

She shrugged a little, implying it should have been obvious, "We were, you know, a couple. A few years ago, but we're still friends. I know I can always crash here when I need to."

Conrad stared at her. She was effortlessly beautiful, easily at least twenty years Freddie's junior, and, as affable as Freddie had been, even the most charitable person couldn't have described him as attractive. He'd had a full beard for as long as Conrad had known him but rather than giving him any sort of disheveled charm, even that had somehow emphasized the weak-chinned, pop-eyed face beneath.

She smiled, the smile of a lost cause, and said, "You wouldn't be the first to be surprised, but I liked him from the moment I met him. There's something sexy about him."

"I'll take it on faith."

She didn't appear to understand the phrase, looking at him with her head cocked before saying, "What about you? How do you know him . . . I'm sorry, what did you say your name was?"

Anyone else would have been offended by the implication—she thought Freddie was sexy but couldn't remember Conrad's name. He laughed to himself as he said, "Conrad. And I knew him through business."

"Conrad," she said, turning the name over.

"Yeah, look, I don't think he'll be coming back."

"Really?" She looked disappointed, even desperate, suggesting Freddie had represented more of a lifeline to her than a place to crash every now and then.

"Maybe. I don't know. Look, wait here while I check something."

He walked into the kitchen, then into the pantry and tapped in the code on the door that led into the storeroom. The light came on automatically but it had been emptied. There hadn't been enough time to clear the house of furniture, but there wasn't a gun or a bullet left in the place.

He'd had a lot of time to think on the journey up from Milan, and even though he'd been hopeful of finding Freddie still here it didn't surprise him to find the place cleaned out. He was clearly up against a complex organization, and whether or not the key players knew about his involvement they'd responded to Frank's death by shutting down his entire operation.

Then there were the two women. The way things were going, he wouldn't have been shocked to discover both were part of it. It was regrettable because he'd liked Alice Benning, but the farther away he got from her, the more convinced he became that she'd been a plant, put on that train to tail him or lead him into a trap.

As for Delphine, his instinct said otherwise. He couldn't pin it down, but whereas Alice had jarred in the details, Delphine came across as effortlessly authentic, even in her eccentric taste in men. And nothing she'd said or done so far had been too polished or convenient.

When he walked back out she'd gone from the hallway, but he could hear some noise above and climbed the stairs to find her in Freddie's bedroom up on the third floor. He'd never been in there before and was surprised by how chintzy it was, and by how tidy—as far as he knew, there wasn't a housekeeper and there had certainly never been any woman in his life that Conrad had met. Still, Delphine was proof that he probably knew as little about Freddie as Freddie had known about him.

She was looking through his wardrobe, a couple of drawers open in a tall chest behind her. She turned when he came in and said, "None of his things have gone. Look, he would have taken clothes, a bag, something." She walked into the bathroom without waiting for a response and said confidently, "He'll be back. His toothbrush is still here, everything."

Conrad thought of the storeroom. He didn't want to tell her what he knew, but before he could think of how to deal with the situation he realized she'd frozen and was looking across the room in horror. He followed the direction of her gaze. For a moment, he couldn't see what she was looking at and then he saw the blood on the pillow and what looked like a faint spatter of blood running up the wall above the headboard.

He walked over and pulled back the duvet, finding the

sheets underneath bloodstained. It was just one more variable, making it even harder for him to decipher what was going on.

He turned and looked at Delphine. She was standing as if mesmerized by the pattern of blood on the sheets, her expression one of horror and disbelief. Belatedly, he pulled the duvet back over it, covering the pillow, too. He didn't know what to say to her.

She seemed to be holding it together and sounded confused and only slightly distraught as she said, "But why?"

"I don't know." Surely though, this couldn't all be the result of killing Frank. If it wasn't, if he'd chosen to retire just as something big was under way, it was either a piece of spectacularly good or spectacularly bad timing, and he wasn't certain he'd ever know which it was. The only facts he had were that he'd set out to kill four people, but, with the exception of Frank, they were all disappearing or proving themselves phantoms.

Delphine sat on the corner of the bed and buried her head in her hands. He wasn't sure if she was crying, but if so, she was doing it silently, no histrionics. He looked out of the window and down into the street, noting the people he could see.

"What will you do?" She looked up questioningly. "I mean, you were planning to crash here. What will you do?"

"What does it matter what I'll do?" She twisted around to stare at him. "Doesn't this shock you at all? Freddie's been murdered." Her final words were like a plea, imploring him to understand.

"Someone's been hurt. We don't know for sure it was Freddie."

"Who else could it be?" He didn't answer because he didn't know, but she said accusingly, "You know! Something's going on and you know about it. What's happened to Freddie?"

He didn't know how to respond, then said simply, "Why would I have come here if I knew what was going on?"

She didn't say anything, and he looked out of the window again, drawn immediately to a young guy standing in a doorway a short distance along the street, talking on a mobile phone. He was wearing jeans and pale Timberland boots, a dark padded jacket. There was something about his dress and his clean-cut looks that marked him out as an American tourist.

But studying him, Conrad was certain he'd seen the guy earlier, either en route from the hotel or as he'd checked out the people on the street before knocking on Freddie's door. He couldn't pinpoint the moment, but he'd seen him, and now the guy was looking like a tourist without behaving like one.

"Delphine, I need you to do something." She looked expectantly. "I want you to leave the house—don't take anything with you—just walk up the street to the right, then after you've turned at least one corner, make like you've forgotten something and come back."

Puzzled and still in shock, she said, "But why, what are you going to do?"

"I'm trying to find out what happened to Freddie. Just trust me on this."

She raised her eyebrows, apparently unable to find a reason not to trust him, and said, "You want me to go now?"

He nodded and Delphine got off the bed and left without

any further questions. Considering she was wearing hiking boots, he couldn't hear her on the stairs. He was looking out the window as the door opened below thirty seconds later.

The guy said something abrupt into his phone and put it away, but he remained leaning casually against the doorway, as if waiting for a friend. Delphine appeared not to notice him. He didn't look at her, either, but once she'd walked past he glanced after her before turning his attention back to the house.

So he wasn't following her, which left three possibilities. He was with the people who'd shut down Gaddi and Fischer and was watching the house to see who showed up there. Or he was working for someone else, watching the house in case the people who'd killed Freddie returned. Or finally, no matter who he was working for, he was watching Conrad.

Delphine was away longer than Conrad had expected, but he smiled when she reappeared because she was carrying pastries and bread. He heard the key in the lock, the door opening and closing, then the same stealth on the stairs before she came back into the bedroom.

He nodded toward the food and said, "Nice touch, I should have thought of that."

"I'm hungry," she said, and took a bite out of one of the pastries.

"It was still a nice touch. Give me your key."

She hesitated, swallowing the pastry before saying, "Tell me first. Why did you have me walk along the street? Where are you going?"

He waved her over to the window. "See that guy down there? He's either watching the house or me or you. I just ruled out you, now I want to rule out me."

Silently, she took the key out and handed it to him, but as he took it she clasped her hand around his and said, "I know what Freddie did. I know how he made his money. I still think we should call the police."

"Give me ten minutes and you can call anyone you like."

Conrad headed downstairs, but before opening the door, he took his gun from his rucksack and slipped it into the inside pocket of his coat. The guy was leaning nonchalantly in the doorway as before, but Conrad focused on the street as he walked past, looking out for other people. At the moment there were just two middle-aged women walking ahead of him, deep in conversation.

He turned a corner and stopped, waited a second, and turned back. As he came back around the corner the guy was walking toward it. He should have been disappointed but in that moment he was triumphant, because he felt like he was playing and beating these people on their own ground.

The guy's pace was thrown for a second but he recovered quickly and did a good impression of someone who just happened to be heading that way. If this was the level of professionalism he was up against, he felt he had even more reason to be confident.

The guy avoided Conrad's gaze, pretending to look at the buildings, and that was what Conrad used against him. As they crossed paths, Conrad drew his gun and pushed it into the padding of the guy's jacket at the same time as he pulled him around by the arm.

"There's no one on the street—I'll drop you right here. Now walk. *Verstehen?*" The final word of German was an afterthought, a precaution in case the guy he'd perceived to be an American tourist turned out to be a local. But he needn't have doubted himself.

"I understand. I'm an American," he said urgently. "Please, don't do anything stupid."

Conrad didn't respond, pushing him back toward the house, even though it was the subtle pressure of the silencer that was propelling him. The guy was even more clean-cut up close, dark blond hair cut so short around the back and sides that Conrad could see the map of his skull, a brand-new look about his clothes, not even a promise of stubble on his face.

There was something of the military man about him, and Conrad thought the guy might try something as he opened the door, but he was surprisingly compliant. Conrad pushed him into the dining room.

"Sit down. Hands on the table." The guy did as he was told. He guessed the right thing to do would have been to check for a gun, but the American could hardly go for a shoulder holster through a zipped jacket. And given that Conrad had no experience at this kind of thing, he guessed he'd probably be more likely to mess up attempting a search. "If you spin me a line about being a tourist I'll shoot you right now."

The guy nodded and said, "My name's Mark Fox, I'm . . . I work for the U.S. government."

"It's funny, I've spoken to one American in ten years and suddenly I seem to be bumping into them everywhere." Either Fox didn't understand or didn't know how to respond because he remained silent. "So what's going on, Mark? What's happening with Frank Dillon and Fabio Gaddi, Eberhardt, our friend Freddie? Start wherever you like, but I want some answers."

He shook his head. "Mr. Hirst, I've heard the name of Frank Dillon, but I don't know anything about him and I don't recognize those other names. All I know is I was drafted in at short notice to come here. I'm based in Berlin—this isn't even my section."

"What were your orders?"

"I was told you might come here."

Conrad was having trouble working this out. He'd begun to suspect on and off that a government might be involved, and the Americans made as much sense as any. But even if they'd had Frank's business dealings under surveillance, he couldn't understand what interest they'd have in following him.

He was casting around for the next question when Delphine appeared in the doorway and before he could say any more she said angrily, "What have you done with Freddie?"

Fox looked at her, then back at Conrad, confused. "I don't know who Freddie is. I swear to God, I have no reason to lie about this."

"Freddie's the man whose dining table you're sitting at. And looking at his bed, I'd say someone killed him quite recently and disposed of the body. So I imagine what Delphine is asking is whether you or the U.S. government had anything to do with it."

Fox shook his head emphatically, saying, "Absolutely not. Look, I was told you might come to this house, but I wasn't told anything about this Freddie guy or about any woman. I was told . . ."

"Who told you?"

He looked questioningly at Conrad, as if speaking to him in code. It was almost as if he thought Conrad was only playing at ignorance for Delphine's benefit. Finally, like it was something he really shouldn't have needed to spell out, he said, "Bill Rutherford. Well, not directly, but that's where the orders came from. I mean, who else would it be?" The name meant nothing to Conrad, but he felt he'd lose the initiative somehow if he asked who Rutherford was.

"Go on. Tell me about the orders."

It worked, because Fox shrugged, at a loss to the purpose of the mind game he was being coerced into, and then said, "Look, all I know is, I was told to come to Lindau in case you showed up here. Then this morning they called and said you were at the Bayerischer Hof. I followed you from there to here."

"And?"

"And nothing," he said, a touch of exasperation creeping into his voice. "I was just told to keep you under surveillance. I was told not to attempt to apprehend you unless absolutely necessary, that you were . . . that you were dangerous."

His hesitancy suggested exactly how dangerous he believed Conrad to be, enough that to verbalize it was sufficient in itself to invoke a violent response. Conrad was happy to let it ride, too, if it meant Fox was more likely to answer his questions as a result.

Delphine had been standing in the same spot, looking on with a blank expression, but she became suddenly animated now, walking into the room and staring at Fox.

"Why is he dangerous?"

"I don't know."

"You didn't ask, you weren't even curious? They sent you here to follow him and you didn't want to know how he was dangerous? That's ridiculous, no?" It was a good point, one that hadn't even occurred to Conrad.

Fox looked ill at ease. "I'd seen his file. It was all I needed to know, and that's how we operate, on a need to know."

Delphine persisted, saying, "So tell me—because I need to know—what was in his file? Why is he so dangerous? Why are you so happy to answer all his questions? It's not normal, I assume, for U.S. government agents to answer questions from anyone with a gun. It's not how you're trained. No?" She was good in a politically indignant French way, and Fox shook his head. "So why do you answer?"

Fox sat in silence, looking at the table, so Conrad said, "I'd like to know about that, too. What does it say in my file?" Even as he asked the question, he felt like he was outside of his own body, trying to find enough distance to take in these simple but disturbing facts, that his every movement was being fairly precisely monitored, that they knew where he'd be heading, that the U.S. government kept a file on him. And in the background, he could hear a mantra-like echo of Frank's voice—*I lied, about everything.*

Reluctantly, Fox said, "Less than it does in most people's. A lot of it's classified. But it says you've killed people."

Delphine looked at Conrad, as if wanting him to deny it. She'd met him less than an hour ago and already she was hoping not to be disappointed. Or maybe she was thinking of the scene in Freddie's bedroom, wondering whether she could be entirely certain that he wasn't responsible for it.

"Well, it's right about that. I've killed people, and you're not telling me anything useful."

"I'm telling you everything I know. The rest is just hearsay . . ." Conrad looked expectantly, and Fox continued as if trying to distance himself from what he was saying, and even from the organization he worked for. "You know how it is with rumors. It means nothing, but the word is—I mean—

79

what they're saying is that you've gone bad, that you've become a rogue agent."

It took Conrad a second or two to answer because he didn't understand at first what Fox had said, as if he'd been speaking in Conrad's second or third language. "What are you talking about? A rogue agent?" He thought of something Klemperer had said to him in Chur, and before Fox could answer, he said, "This file they have on me, who does it say I work for?"

Fox looked like he was being subjected to some new and unorthodox interrogation technique. He looked at Delphine, as if hoping she'd see his confusion and intervene, and said, "I don't understand. What . . . ?"

Conrad cut in sharply. "*Who* do I work for?"

Fox finally boiled over and in a moment of confusion and temper, he blurted out, "I don't know what you want from me, man! You're one of us! I don't understand what you want me to say. You're one of us!"

Conrad still didn't get what he was saying, but Delphine was ahead of him and, quiet and measured, she said, "And by 'one of us,' you mean?"

He looked at her, almost apologetic as he said, "I don't know what kind of mix-up has gone on here, but there *has* been a misunderstanding. I'm with the CIA, we both are."

He turned and stared directly at Conrad, as if challenging him to deny it.

"I'm with the CIA?" Fox didn't answer, and looked irritated that he was being asked to restate the record.

Fox thought he was telling the truth, that much was clear, but it was a lie, and it was the nature of the lie that angered him so much. He couldn't understand why they were doing

it, except that it was probably convenient for him to be painted as a rogue agent who needed to be eliminated—even then,
until now, no one had actually tried to kill him. He looked at
Fox and said, "You're forgetting something, Mark."

Fatigued, Fox said, "What?"

"I'm English."

Conrad shot him in the head, a neat hole that spurted
blood almost the full length of the table. Fox was short
and stocky enough that he didn't fall forward, but his head
slumped and then he fell sideways off the chair. Delphine
was staring at the body and the table as if trying to work out
what she'd just seen, as if she was convinced it was a stunt
or a magic trick.

After a few seconds, she turned to Conrad and said in a
strangely fragile voice, "You killed him?" Conrad nodded.
"But why?"

Conrad thought about it. He hadn't needed a reason and
wasn't sure he could give her one. Whether or not Fox had
been telling the truth, he'd told him everything he was going
to tell him. If the things he'd told him contained even ele-
ments of the truth it probably wouldn't have hurt to keep
him alive, but nor did it hurt to kill him.

Maybe he was just angry at being lied to, at being a
pawn. Maybe he'd shot Fox because he couldn't kill Frank
again, because his Eberhardt was a myth, because Gaddi and
Fischer had disappeared. Maybe he'd killed him because it
was the easiest way of ending the conversation.

"I don't know. I just did."

She nodded slowly, taking in the naked inadequacy of
his answer, then swayed a little and crumpled to the floor as
suddenly as if she'd been hit by a bullet herself. If there was

any room for doubt that she was the innocent bystander she appeared, it was gone now. He almost felt bad for killing Fox in front of her, for not sparing her from the bad dreams that would inevitably follow.

He put his gun back into his rucksack, slung it over his shoulder, and then lifted her up onto her feet. She was slim, but her body had that same soft tactile quality he'd felt in her hands. He could imagine men finding themselves just wanting to hold her, to take comfort in her warmth. He could imagine it, and even now, even after these setbacks, he still hoped the day would come when he might actually feel like that, too.

She came around enough for him to guide her through into the kitchen, just about the only part of the house that wasn't tainted by death in some way. She was groggy and disoriented, mumbling to herself in French. He sat her in a chair at the kitchen table, found some apple brandy in a cupboard, and poured a glass.

By the time he returned with the drink, she'd revived enough to be staring at him. She took the drink from him and sipped at it absentmindedly. Her voice was spilling over with emotion as she said, "I don't understand why you killed him. He said you both work for the CIA."

"He was lying, or wrong. I'd know if I worked for the CIA." Yet even as he said it, he realized the only thing he knew for certain was that he hadn't been working for a German crime boss all this time.

"But you still had no reason to kill him."

"I know." He tried to find regret, that same regret he'd felt after killing Klemperer. Perhaps it would come in time. "I probably shouldn't have killed him. I just did."

Saying the words made him realize how inadequate his

reasons were, for everything, even for the way he'd crashed and burned in the first place. The girl he'd loved had been killed, and he'd somehow used that, in his own mind at least, to justify his descent into madness and violence. Touched by death, he'd carried it like plague into the homes of his targets all over Europe, and he knew that no loss could ever mitigate a fall like that.

"Will you kill me?"

He understood now that she wasn't just emotional, but scared. And it was a relief to know that he could reassure her, that there would be no point in killing her because his identity and his past were, it seemed, less of a secret than he'd ever imagined or planned for.

"I won't kill you. All I want is to quit. It's just proving more complicated than I'd hoped."

"You want to quit?" Her tone suggested it had been an extraordinary statement.

"That's what I said. I don't want to kill people any-more."

"But that's what I don't understand." She stopped herself, took a gulp of brandy, bracing against its rough edges, and said, "I don't understand a lot of things. For one, if you don't want to kill people anymore, you could start by not killing people, particularly for no reason." She stared at him, and he came close to laughing as he realized she was waiting for him to make some sort of pledge to that end. He nodded and she appeared to weigh his sincerity before continuing. "But if you're so certain you don't work for the CIA, yet you're determined to quit, who do you think you work for? You must have been working for someone if you think of quitting from them."

"It's complicated." She looked expectantly. He hesitated, then grabbed the bottle of apple brandy and another glass and sat across the table from her. He poured himself a drink, and Delphine reached out and took the bottle, adding a little more to her own glass. He took a good gulp, swirling its heat around his mouth to take the sting out of it—he wouldn't have even used it in cooking, but he had a feeling that was what Freddie must have used it for. "For the last nine years, I've been working freelance for a German crime boss. My contact point was a guy called Frank Dillon."

"The man he knew?"

"The man he said he'd heard of," said Conrad, correcting her. "A couple of weeks ago, I decided to quit."

"Why?"

It was liberating to be telling someone about this, now that none of it mattered, even more liberating than talking about his deeper past to Alice Benning on the train. Even so, there were still limits on what he was willing to share with her.

"Personal reasons," he said. She looked like she might pressure him but changed her mind and shrugged. "As far as I knew, there were only four people who knew what I'd been doing all these years, and because I know the crime world, or thought I knew the crime world, I knew that getting out could be difficult, even dangerous. So I decided to kill those four people." He thought she might object to his logic and added quickly, "You have to understand, these people won't ever let someone just walk away. As long as I'm alive, I'd be a liability—it's easier for them to play safe and kill me. I know, because I've killed people in exactly those circumstances. So you see, killing those final four people was my insurance policy."

She was lifting her glass to her lips but stopped and put it back on the table, suspicious again as she asked, "Was Freddie one of those people?"

"Yes, he was. But I didn't kill him."

"But that's why you came here today."

He nodded, qualifying it by saying, "I don't know, things had already started to go wrong. I wanted to speak to him more than anything, but, yeah, I probably would have killed him. See, I killed Frank, but one of the others has disappeared, I'm guessing Freddie's dead, and the crime boss . . ."

"What?"

He had no reason to feel awkward about being amateurish—he *was* an amateur by most measures—but he was still reluctant to expose the bare bones of his gullibility. He thought out his words carefully before saying, "I met this guy nine years ago. I was malleable." The word confused her. "No, that's wrong anyway. My mind wasn't right. I'd been fighting in Yugoslavia."

Surprised, she said, "You were in Yugoslavia?"

"For a while. Anyway, I was willing to kill for them, that was the important thing, and I didn't ask questions. I've been invisible for nine years and that suited them. I even thought it suited me. The thing is, when I tracked down the crime boss, it wasn't the man I met nine years ago."

She finally took that interrupted sip from her brandy and said, "So you have to accept that he, the man you just killed, might have been telling the truth. You must have been working for somebody, and he knew the name of Frank . . . ?"

"Dillon."

"So it's possible, no? You know, it's not without precedence. That's the correct word?" He nodded. "The CIA, they use foreign prisons, they use foreign torturers—it's in the newspapers. So they use foreigners to kill people, too. It's like, you haven't been in the CIA, because you would know that, sure, but you've been working for them. Possibly they didn't want you to know."

There was a reasonable chance she was right, and if it was true, in some small way, it legitimized what he'd been doing all these years. But it didn't make him feel any better. Maybe he'd been doing the work of the Free World, but he'd preferred it when he'd thought he was a criminal—not least because any questions of guilt and atonement were cleaner cut that way.

He also had an uneasy feeling that the Free World might be even less keen to see him on the loose than Eberhardt would have been. If Fox had been telling him the truth, the idea of killing four people and being free was beginning to look more than a little delusional.

"I need to go." He got up and walked into the dining room to get Fox's SIM card and ID.

Delphine looked alarmed and got up too, calling after him, "Where?"

"Back to my hotel. After that, I have no idea. I need to think."

"What about me?"

"I told you I wouldn't kill you."

"No, I mean . . ." She looked a little embarrassed. "I haven't got any money. That's why I came to crash here, but I can't stay here now."

Conrad looked down at Fox and thought of the blood-stained bed upstairs. He supposed the right thing to do was to tell her that it was too dangerous for her to be with him, that she needed to get as far away from him as possible, but this wasn't a film and she was an adult.

"I'll tell reception that my girlfriend might be arriving. Wait here for an hour, or go for a coffee somewhere, then come to the hotel—the Bayerischer Hof."

She nodded acknowledgment to his instructions, then said with an afterthought, "I didn't catch your surname."

"Hirst. My name is Conrad Hirst." And right now, that was about the only fact of which he could be absolutely certain.

8

HE didn't think she'd call the police, but he didn't think she'd come, either. No matter how little money she had, he reckoned she'd find some way out of Lindau once she'd had time to reflect on what had happened at Freddie's house, and what all those stray facts she'd acquired about Conrad amounted to.

He moved one of the chairs so that he could sit overlooking the terrace. The mist had never lifted and it was getting dark now, but he could see hazily diffused lights here and there down below. If it weren't for the fact that his cover was already blown, he could have happily stayed there forever, or at least until the money ran out—twenty years, possibly more?

But far from being blown, his cover had been as much an illusion as everything else. He thought back on his ingenious flight from Milan and laughed at himself, knowing now that they'd covered all points in advance, knowing also that "they" were the most powerful intelligence agency in the world.

He wouldn't run. It was undoubtedly possible—half the world's terrorists proved it—but he didn't want to live like that. He'd lost one decade of his life, he wouldn't spend the next two or three living like a war criminal, moving on every time anyone got too close. He'd experienced enough to know that survival wasn't an end in itself, that it was better to die trying to live than not live at all.

He shouldn't have killed Fox, he appreciated that too late. He could have used him as a go-between, to find out what the CIA wanted from him, to find out if this was all in response to Frank's death, if it was all connected. Above all, he could have used Fox to find out if they'd be willing to let him go.

But he sensed he knew the answer to that question already. In truth, the only plan open to him was to go home and wait for them to make a move. He couldn't take on the CIA. But thinking of that, realizing that they probably would dispose of him, simply reinforced his earlier determination to carry out just one more of the four deaths he'd originally planned.

Nine years ago he'd met a man calling himself Julius Eberhardt. If Fox had been telling the truth, "Eberhardt" had been with the CIA, and for all Conrad knew, still was. Possibly he was Bill Rutherford, the man Fox had mentioned, expecting Conrad to recognize the name. If nothing else, Conrad knew that he had to kill that other Eberhardt, because it was right and fitting, because he couldn't go back nine years and kill him in his little room at Die Alpenrose.

The telephone rang and Conrad picked up to the receptionist.

"Good evening, Mr. Hirst. There's a Miss Racette in reception. She claims that she is your girlfriend and that you're expecting her."

He smiled to himself, massively relieved and unsure why. Sternly, he said, "She is indeed, and I specifically informed the reception desk that she'd be arriving this evening."

"I understand. Please accept my apologies, Mr. Hirst."

He hung up and waited impatiently for her to arrive. When the door opened, there was a porter carrying her backpack. Conrad tipped him and once they were alone she smiled, offering a little shrug, an implicit suggestion that she knew this wasn't the smart move.

"Why did you come?"

She shrugged again, bigger this time, as if asking why anyone did anything. There was a sofa facing the end of the bed and she slumped down onto it before saying, "I don't know. I started walking to the railway station, you know, but I couldn't leave, even after what I saw you do." She laughed a little, embarrassed, perhaps still in shock. "I thought I might be able to help."

"Why would you want to help me?"

"I kept asking myself that question all the way back here, and I still don't know the answer."

"But here you are."

"Yes, here I am."

"Well, thanks for the sentiment, but I don't see how you can help, not unless you're friends with the head of the CIA."

She leaned forward eagerly, as if about to admit to exactly that, but said, "That's what I was thinking. You need to think of the people you've killed, think of who they were. There must be a pattern."

He walked over and sat on the end of the bed opposite her. "I've killed a lot of people. Some of them could have been political. But some of them . . ." He shook his head. "Trade union people, businessmen, an agent for football players, nightclub owners—I can't see these being the kind of people the CIA would want to eliminate. And thinking of it, even if they did, why didn't they do it in-house? Isn't that what people like Fox are for?"

She untied her boots and took them off as she said, "I don't know. But you must think about the political ones, recent especially."

"Because?"

"Because that could explain what this is all about. You think this—Freddie and these other men disappearing—you think it's all because you killed the first man, because you tried to quit, but what if these things have happened at the same time by coincidence only? That's why you have to look at the murders you've performed, because one of them might help you now."

He'd killed four people for Frank this year. Two had been businessmen, the third had been a Muslim school teacher, the fourth had been Hans Klemperer. In retrospect, all of them could have been political assassinations, though at the time he'd only considered the Klemperer job off his usual ground.

"The most recent job I did—even at the time I thought it was Eberhardt getting rid of someone in exchange for political favors. It was an old man, a Cold War veteran who'd written his memoirs."

She smiled, as if they were getting somewhere, and said, "So they think you have his memoirs."

He shook his head. "No, I had to send the disks to an address in Zurich and I did that." He thought of the duplicates, sitting in the bank with the disks he'd taken from Frank, but he didn't want to tell her, and he didn't want to talk about the Klemperer job anymore. Thinking about Klemperer reminded him of his reasons for wanting to quit, something that could only depress him now, with the hope of success evaporating. The only hope left to him was that of going out in style.

"Okay, not the disks. They think the old man told you something?"

"Even if that's true, I can't see how it helps me to know that. Look, I took disks from Frank Dillon's house—chances are, that's what they want from me."

"Or the disks are the only reason you're still alive. It's how it is in the cinema, always."

"Sure." He looked at his watch, bored even by the subject of his own fate. "Shall we go down for dinner?"

She looked at her backpack and said, "I have no nice clothes with me. We can have dinner here, no?"

They ordered dinner and ate in the room. She was a good conversationalist, but even though she seemed curious about him, about his childhood, Yugoslavia, the same things that had occupied him on the train to Milan, he couldn't muster answers for her the way he had for Alice Benning.

Was it because of the way he now perceived that earlier conversation, as a fishing expedition by a CIA agent? Or was it that there'd been a spark with Alice—even if she had been lying to him, though a part of him still refused to believe that, clinging stubbornly to the idea that she'd been exactly what she'd claimed, a journalist. In the end, he supposed the novelty of talking about himself had simply worn off.

So, instead, he asked her how she knew Freddie, what she did. In answering, she volunteered plenty of information about her own childhood, extensive details about another boyfriend and a brief account of her doctorate in international relations. She was thinking of abandoning it, which had been part of the reason for this trip.

Occasionally, she drifted back to his current predicament, but he steered her away from it. If he thought about it, he'd begin to question her, wondering why she was here, wondering if she was genuine, and there was no need for any of that. For the first time in many years he was sitting having dinner with someone, the setting intimate, the conversation relaxed, on her part at least, and he wanted to enjoy that without any subtext.

They had a bottle of wine with dinner and, afterward, he ordered a couple of large cognacs from the bar and they took them out onto the terrace. She was shivering standing out there but she linked her arm through his and seemed intent on staying.

"Isn't this beautiful?"

"Yes it is," he said, warming to her more with that question than he had with anything else she'd said all day, because there was nothing to see. The mist had thickened and clung to the hotel now, damp on their faces, blanketing even the darkness. It was as if they were hidden away, as if no one would ever find them for as long as the mist held.

"When I was little, where my cousins lived, they would sometimes get cut off by the snow in the winter, and living in Paris, I would be so envious. Of course, as we got older, they envied me for living in the city."

He nodded, thinking back to Birkenstein a few days earlier, and said, "I like the idea of living in a place that gets snowed in."

"You live in England now?"

"Luxembourg City, as much as I live anywhere. It looks like the time's coming for me to move." Of course, like Frank, like Klemperer and Freddie, he might well have left his thoughts of moving just a little too late. But if he survived, he would move on, not because he didn't like Luxembourg, but because he no longer liked what it represented in his life.

At the end of the evening, she dragged her backpack into the bathroom. He heard the shower running and when she came back out, she was wearing only a long T-shirt. She put the backpack against the wall and walked over to the bed.

Conrad had been standing looking out the window at the mist and the subdued reflection of the room behind him, but he turned as she walked over, realizing how long her legs were now, taking in the way the fabric of the T-shirt hung on her breasts.

She looked hesitant as she reached the bed, and sounded embarrassed as she said, "It sounds crazy, but I've had a really great evening."

"Why is it crazy?"

She looked nonplussed and said, "Because of today. You know, today was frightening and . . . overwhelming."

"Of course," he said, reminding himself that few other people were as blasé about death and killing as he was. This had probably been the most shocking day of Delphine's life and, now that he thought about it, he hoped she'd never have another like it.

"What I mean to say is, I've had a great evening, and I'm

grateful to you, Conrad, but I don't want you to think I'm the kind of woman who . . ."

He'd wanted nothing from her, but he couldn't help but feel snubbed.

"Of course. I'll sleep on the sofa."

"No," she said insistently. "I don't mean that. We can share the bed. I just wanted you to understand . . ."

"That we're only sharing the bed," he offered helpfully.

She smiled, apparently happy that he understood, and said, "Exactly."

"Don't worry, Delphine, I'm not really that kind of man, either." If he were, he'd probably be questioning her unwillingness to sleep with him when she listed Freddie Fischer among her ex-partners.

He stripped down to his boxers, got into bed, and turned the light out a few seconds later. He could sense her lying nearby, but at first they were both silent. Then she turned toward him and said quietly, "What will you do tomorrow?"

He was staring up at the ceiling as he answered. "I don't know. I suppose I'll go back to Luxembourg. They seem to know where I am anyway, so I might as well be at home." The word "home" lingered in the silence and made him think of a game he'd played as a child, repeating a word again and again until it became meaningless.

A little while later, she said, "You think you'll be in danger?"

"I don't know. I really don't know. If it is Frank's disks they want, well, they'll just have to come to my apartment and ask for them. If they just want to get rid of me, fair enough, but I'll take a few of them down with me." He was thinking of one in particular, of course: the fake Eberhardt.

She moved a little closer to him, the heat of her breath just finding his neck as she said, "I want to come with you."

"Why would you do that?" He waited a couple of beats for her to respond, then said, "I'll buy you a ticket to wherever you need to go. I just can't see why you would want to come with me."

"Can't you?" He heard her turn onto her back and immediately missed the warmth of her. "Actually, I'm not sure why I would want to come, either. I just do."

He had no idea how much danger he was in, if any at all, but he clearly hadn't spelled it out properly to Delphine. There was something about her, though, something strong and daring, the strident way she'd talked to Fox, that made Conrad think she'd have wanted to go with him no matter what the risks.

"Okay, if you want to come, you can."

"Good," she said and turned again toward him, this time draping her arm across his chest, resting her leg against his. It was a shock after all this time, the contact of flesh, the comfort and intimacy of having someone hold onto him.

It confused him too, and left him wondering whether she was simply snuggling down or whether she was expecting him to respond. He hadn't lived enough to know what she wanted of him, and even if he had known, he wasn't sure he could provide it.

In some disjointed way he was conscious of her scent, of the warm smoothness of her leg pressing against his, of her hand rising and falling softly with his chest. He was conscious of her breath and visualized how easy it would be to turn onto his side and find her mouth with his, how easy to become lost in the touch of her body.

Yet he remained motionless, and for all his ability to think himself into her arms, there was no twinge of adrenaline, no hint of a sexual urge. He remained still and so did she and he listened as her breathing became shallower and was relieved when finally she seemed to sleep.

So she wouldn't find out yet, if at all, that what she'd seen today was just the surface of how damaged he was, how inhuman. She wouldn't find out that she was holding onto a dead man, stitched and embalmed, his warmth residual, his movements merely the final tricks of a spent nervous system.

It didn't matter what kind of woman Delphine was, or how beautiful, how sensual—there would probably never be anything here for her. It was simply a lost language to him.

Conrad Hirst

I think only you would understand and not see me as some kind of petrified freak. There hasn't been anyone in these ten years, no one at all. I don't just mean there hasn't been a relationship, that I haven't dated, I mean I haven't touched a woman in all that time—I never picked up a girl in a hotel bar, never sought the solace of prostitutes. What solace could there be in that, anyway?

I know you would understand, I always knew. But I don't think anyone else could. My relationship with you, viewed from the outside, would have amounted to nothing. It was the shortest relationship of my life, by a long shot, and you were only my fourth girlfriend. I smile even using that word, because we were together for so few weeks that I don't think we ever got around to referring to each other in that way. Did you ever tell anyone I was your boyfriend, your lover? Did we feel the need to tell anyone anything about us at all?

We knew what those weeks were, but others would understandably question my willingness to abandon the search to replace you even before it had begun. What insanity could lie behind such an obstinate refusal to move on? And to all of them, I would say, "You didn't know her, how can you judge me when you didn't even know her?"

Maybe a psychiatrist would suggest that it was about more than you. And I grant that other things might have played a part in the way I am. If I'd run any other way that night, if I hadn't found a refuge in horror, maybe things would have been different.

But even if things had turned out differently, if I hadn't compounded the damage, if I'd found someone else, I would never have felt the same. And at this moment in time, I hardly care if I don't touch a woman for another ten years or ever again. Because that woman cannot be you.

I love you,
Conrad

HE'D been up early, taken breakfast downstairs and walked around the island for an hour. The mist had evaporated into a faultless blue within an hour of sunrise, and it was as warm as it had been a few weeks before in Chur. The streets of the two towns even looked similar—the same muted pastels of the high, narrow merchants' houses, the same cobbled streets—and that filled him with a renewed sense of what this was all about, why his life had changed.

By the time he got back to the room, Delphine was in the shower. She'd straightened the bedding and flung the windows open onto the terrace so the room was already light and fresh. It hardly looked like two people had slept there.

But then, he hadn't slept much anyway. He'd looked up at the dark ceiling most of the night, simultaneously comforted by her touch and reminded how far away he was from her and everyone else. That had made him think of Fox, too, because it was only in the warmth and stillness of the bed, only with a virtual stranger lying next to him, that he'd remembered Fox had been wearing a wedding band.

There was a young wife out there, perhaps even a young family. He imagined them now, waking up to this sunny day, not knowing yet that their husband and father was dead. And it troubled Conrad to know that, as well as the first hint of regret for Fox's pointless death, he also felt a slither of spiteful satisfaction.

He heard her turn off the shower, so he called out, "I'm back."

"Good morning!" Shortly afterward, she came out wearing one of the robes, drying her hair with a towel. "You were up early." She smiled and kissed him on both cheeks.

She was still sultry and beautiful in a bathrobe, just as she had been sleeping. It made him wistful, though, thinking of Anneke. She'd looked terrible in the mornings, puffy and mussed up and still half subdued by sleep, but he'd loved that about her. She'd joked once about it being a glimpse of her future, and he'd loved that, too.

At twenty-two, he'd already been so in love with her he'd happily imagined them spending the rest of their lives together. And even now, looking back over a distance of ten years, it didn't seem an immature or reckless dream.

There was a knock on the door and they both looked. He turned back to her and said, "Did you order breakfast?"

She shook her head and he went and looked through the spyhole. There were two men in suits, one of them with a mustache, both looking official. In some hotel or other, he'd once watched an old German cop drama, not understanding a word of it, but the men he could see through the spyhole looked remarkably like the lead characters. He opened the top of his rucksack and hung it on the back of the door before opening.

Both men showed him ID, and the one with the mustache said, "Mr. Hirst, could we talk with you, please? My name is Carl Hoeffler, my colleague is Dieter Korn, we're Criminal Intelligence Officers with Interpol."

Interpol. One outcome he'd never contemplated was being arrested and going to prison, perhaps for the rest of his life. His first instinct was to think the CIA had alerted them, but from what little he knew from newspapers and television, the CIA took care of its own business and, if anything, wouldn't have wanted a rival organization like Interpol becoming involved.

That, in turn, made him see this could be a lucky break. If Interpol had been tracking him independently, maybe so had others, and that could only make it harder for the CIA to dispose of him. Bizarrely, things had gone full circle, and it was possible now that the more people who knew who he was, the safer he'd be.

It was just as well, too, because it seemed his name was increasingly common currency, so much so that it made the events and intentions of the last week laughable.

Conrad stood back and let them in. Both men were surprised to see Delphine standing there and Hoeffler immediately turned and said, "I'm sorry, I didn't realize you had a companion. We need to discuss some matters with you in private."

"It's not a problem, we'll go out onto the terrace. Would you like tea or coffee?"

Korn looked ready to accept, but Hoeffler threw him a look and said to Conrad, "Thank you, but no. We won't keep you very long. Please?" Hoeffler wasn't talking like a man who was about to arrest him.

Conrad led the way out onto the terrace, offering them seats before closing the windows. Delphine looked panicked, her face asking a question he couldn't answer. He shrugged and gave her a smile, trying to reassure her.

He guessed it couldn't be anything to do with what had happened at Freddie's house because surely that would have been a matter for the German police, not Interpol, but beyond that, he had no idea what they wanted from him. Whatever it was, he was beginning to feel more and more at ease, and in surprisingly good spirits, because they had nothing to throw at him and nothing they could take from him.

He sat down and looked across the lake to the Swiss and Austrian Alps.

"Isn't it a glorious day?"

Hoeffler looked at the view, knocked off balance slightly by Conrad's casual tone, and said, "It's very beautiful. If you don't mind, Mr. Hirst, we wish to talk with you about the suicide of Hans Klemperer."

"Wasn't he a composer or a conductor or something?"

"Amusing," said Hoeffler, like it was the least amusing thing he'd ever heard. "We know that Herr Klemperer was murdered some three weeks ago in Chur, Switzerland. It was intended for the murder to look like suicide."

"Obviously not very successfully."

"I can't comment on that, but we have external evidence proving this to be the case."

Conrad glanced at Korn who was looking in through the windows. He followed his gaze and noticed that a naked Delphine was dressing nonchalantly from her backpack just outside the bathroom door.

"Maybe you could ask your colleague to keep his eyes on the road."

Hoeffler didn't understand at first, but then saw what was going on and offered a quick rebuke to Korn in German. Both men looked to be in their late thirties, paunchy, running headlong into middle age, but it was clear that Hoeffler had seniority.

"Now, where were we? A murder in Switzerland. And you want me to tell you . . . what exactly?" He was guessing they knew everything but he wasn't going to make it easy for them, and maybe in the process he'd get them to tell him something he didn't know.

"Mr. Hirst, we know you killed Herr Klemperer. We have all the evidence we need to prove this."

"So why don't you arrest me?" Their opening questions and their behavior made that seem like a remote possibility, but the prospect of spending the next ten to fifteen years in a Swiss prison didn't seem so bad.

Hoeffler reacted as if Conrad had made fun of him, in bad taste at that, and said, "Excuse me?"

"If you have evidence that I killed Klemperer, arrest me."

Korn raised his eyebrows and laughed to himself, apparently taking some pleasure from his colleague's difficulties.

Hoeffler threw him a reproachful glance, and then looked awkward as he said, "We're not here to arrest you, Mr. Hirst, we're here to ask for your assistance. Herr Klemperer had, we believe, written some memoirs. It's why you destroyed the computer."

"A smarter man would have kept duplicate files."

"We know you have them, Mr. Hirst."

"How do you know?" There could only be two answers—either they'd been tipped off by someone involved in the hit, or the house had been bugged.

"I'm not able to give you this information."

"Then I'm not able to assist you. Look, if it's any consolation, I don't know anything about Klemperer or why he was marked. If you need answers, go to the people who employed me."

Hoeffler smiled, like they were finally getting somewhere, and said, "But, Mr. Hirst, that is what we're trying to find out. We know your usual employer didn't send you on this job, we just want to know who did."

"Well, Herr Hoeffler, you might not believe it, but you almost certainly know more about that than I do." And in that, he was being completely honest. They were talking about him having two employers. But even if he now knew that the CIA was one of them, he didn't know which, or the jobs it had sent him on. He stood up, followed by Hoeffler and lazily by Korn. "Let me have your card. If those disks show up, I'll forward them to you."

"Perhaps just one or two more questions . . ." said Hoeffler, apparently unused to having other people decide when an interview was over.

"Who's my regular employer?"

Hoeffler looked uncomfortable, as if he sensed it was beyond his authority to answer that question. It was an alarming revelation for Conrad, because he finally realized what had been so odd about this encounter—they were intimidated by him. They hadn't talked to him like a suspect, but as a person around whom they had to tread very carefully. It was as if he had some sort of diplomatic immunity.

Finally, Hoeffler said, "We understand your official status is very unusual, but it's not my position to discuss it."

"The CIA, right?" Hoeffler remained silent and uncomfortable, his expression confirming that Conrad was right, that Fox had told him the truth, that he'd been working for the CIA all this time, and that Frank had probably been his CIA handler. Fox had also apparently told another truth, because without even knowing it, he *had* become a rogue agent, killing Klemperer for someone else. "Well, let me tell you something, I was never recruited, not properly, and as for my official status, the first I heard that I even worked for the CIA was yesterday afternoon. So how on earth am I meant to know who sent me to kill Klemperer?"

Both men looked astonished. Even Korn, who'd looked bored and distracted until now, suddenly snapped to attention and said in a surprisingly soft voice, "This is true? You didn't know?"

Before he could answer, Hoeffler said, "But who did you think you were working for?"

"I didn't think at all, if truth be told, and I suppose that's why they found me such an attractive proposition. I thought I was working for a German crime boss. Julius Eberhardt?"

"Ah," said Hoeffler, as if he understood the loose connection—maybe they knew about Frank. "This is very interesting."

"It ranks pretty high in the annals of stupidity, doesn't it? I've been a CIA hitman for nine years and I didn't even know about it."

They looked at him for a moment or two, dumbfounded, and then the softly spoken Korn said, "But it's good, yes? You know you're not a criminal now."

Conrad started laughing, a response that confused both of them. Hoeffler interrupted him, saying, "Please, Mr. Hirst, it would be very valuable to us if you were willing to talk some more about your activities, on a strictly informal basis, naturally."

"I'll think about it. I have some things to deal with first. I'll give you my contact details. If you want, you can get in touch in a fortnight or so."

Hoeffler nodded gratefully but said, "It's not necessary, we have your contact details."

"Of course you do," said Conrad. "Is there anybody who doesn't?"

"We'll see ourselves out. Thank you, Mr. Hirst, and good luck."

"Good luck," added Korn with a mix of sympathy and respect. Conrad wasn't entirely sure what entitled him to either.

Conrad took one last look over the lake, then walked in and found Delphine looking baffled, ready to leave.

"Ready?"

"They were Interpol?"

"Yeah, but it wasn't anything to worry about. So, *are* you ready?"

"Of course. And you?"

He nodded, picking up his bag as he said, "Let's get out of here before the profile writer for *The Times* shows up."

She followed him into the corridor, laughing only as she caught up with what he'd said. "You're funny; I didn't expect that, after yesterday."

"Well, I used to be, then I wasn't for a long time. Not sure the timing's great, but I do seem to be rediscovering my sense of humor."

"It suits you."

"Thanks."

But it wasn't the only thing Conrad was rediscovering. He could also feel himself grasping toward a moral framework of sorts. It was still confused, still lost in too many years of not even understanding what it meant to end a life. It would take the rest of his life to come to terms with the wrongs he'd done himself, but the wrongs that had been done *to* him were coming into sharper focus all the time.

Despite what Korn had said, he didn't see his killings as any more legitimate for having been government sanctioned. They were murders, deaths carried out beyond the reach of the law. And the CIA, or at least the people who'd sanctioned his recruitment, who'd handled him, those people deserved some payback for dragging him into it.

His "recruitment" had worked perfectly for them for nine years. But whatever their reasons had been, whatever benefit they'd gained from employing him, the time had come for them to see the dangers of creating someone who wasn't part of the program, who wasn't bound by its rules or protocols, and who was presumably excluded from its pension plan.

10

DELPHINE didn't mention the visit from Interpol again until they were on the train. But once they were cutting around the eastern end of the lake, bound for Zurich, she said, "The men from Interpol, were they asking about Freddie?" He didn't know if Freddie had elderly parents somewhere, or any other family, but if he didn't, probably no one would ask about Freddie ever again, except her.

"No, it was something else." He was reluctant to talk about it, realizing that any of the passengers sitting within earshot could be keeping him under surveillance. But then, given the way Hoeffler and Korn had treated him, it probably wasn't much of a risk. No one was planning to arrest him for what he'd done, and whatever secrets he unwittingly possessed, it didn't really matter to him who found out about them. It was the one distinction Fox had failed to make—he'd worked for the CIA, but he had no personal or professional stake in what it was doing, not even a patriotic duty. "It was about the last job I did."

"See," she said triumphantly. "I told you to think about

your recent jobs. I'm sure that's where you'll find the explanation."

"Maybe." He wasn't entirely convinced there would be an explanation, not one that would make sense to him, at any rate. Still aiming for a little discretion, he said, "They confirmed what Fox said about who was employing me. But they also said that my last job wasn't for them, it was for someone else."

She looked confused and initially he thought he was going to have to spell it out, but she was actually ahead of him. "Your contact, you said his name was Frank?" Conrad nodded. "He always told you that you worked for one person, when you actually worked for another. So, it's possible, no, that he had you also working for other people?"

It was what Hoeffler had suggested. Now that he'd had time to think about it, though, he was less certain. If any of the people he'd killed this year had looked like a CIA target, it was Klemperer, and perhaps the Muslim schoolteacher, too. On the other hand, Frank certainly had it in him to double-cross his own country's intelligence agency.

"I don't know, I think the people I've been working for are probably too sophisticated to allow something like that to happen."

She wasn't going to be so easily swayed and persisted, saying, "Well, ask yourself, the person you—your last job, is it something you could imagine your employers wanting to happen?"

Conrad was getting frustrated edging around key words like this, and he was getting frustrated with her desire to work it all out. It was a game to her, a complex puzzle, and she'd undoubtedly seen films where people did exactly that, but they didn't have the beginnings of a chance at working out what was going on here. And Conrad didn't even want to know, he just wanted to kill the Eberhardt pretender and be left to get on with his life.

"I have absolutely no idea, Delphine. That's why they've employed me all these years, because I have no idea, because I don't know anything and don't want to know anything. His name was Klemperer, German I presume, some kind of Cold War veteran—for all I know, anyone from the CIA to the pope could have wanted him out of the way."

She laughed a little, but said, "I remember now, you told me about him yesterday, the man who'd written his memoirs."

"That's the guy."

"You sent the computer disks somewhere, destroyed his computer."

"That's the one."

"So it's for certain, they either think you have a copy of the memoirs or that the old man told you something." Here she was, talking about the disks again, the disks that Interpol knew he'd taken.

"No, it's not enough. And it doesn't begin to explain the people disappearing, what happened to Freddie, all of that." She was about to offer up an argument but he continued, saying, "This has to be about me deciding to quit, maybe about the disks I took from Frank's house, the rest of it just has to be a coincidence, or peripheral stuff that's come to light because of it. I just can't see this being about an old man's memoirs. It's all too flaky."

"His memoirs got him killed, no?"

"Sure. Writing a book can get you killed, things infinitely

less significant than writing a book can get you killed, but this is something bigger, and a book can't do that."

"I hope you're right." She didn't look hopeful. He couldn't understand why she was so concerned, or why she thought Klemperer's memoirs might be a more troubling underlying problem than having the CIA on his back.

Nor did Delphine seem to be taking in that he was totally ill-equipped to play the detective. Her international relations doctorate probably gave her a better idea of what was going on than he had from being down on the ground. And it was all a distraction to him, anyway—he didn't care about the tangle of connected players and organizations that surrounded him, and had no burning desire to unravel it.

All he wanted was to get back to Luxembourg, to see if he could flush out the people keeping track of him, to kill the ones he wanted to kill and get assurances from the others. Maybe the assurances wouldn't be worth much, but even so, he had a feeling things would be better once he got home, and that he'd find out one way or another whether he would ever have the chance to start again.

Delphine had never been to Luxembourg before and was impressed by the city and its setting. She was even more impressed that Conrad's apartment was in the old town. But he could tell she was disappointed now that she was inside and actually looking at it. She strolled around, nodding approvingly, but it was too cold and male a space for her.

Apart from his once-weekly visits from Rosie, who cleaned and shopped for him, and occasional deliveries, no one else had ever been in the place. Now, for the first time, he was seeing it from a stranger's point of view, the minimalism and lack of clutter teetering on the edge of a complete absence of personality, which was about right if he was honest with himself.

From the sitting room windows, Delphine looked at the building across the street and then turned and said, "It's a great apartment. When did you move in?"

He smiled and said, "I know, it's not exactly full of homely charm. Still, it makes one task easier."

She looked questioningly, but he didn't respond and instead started sweeping the place for bugs or anything else that was suspicious, acutely conscious that he had very little idea what he was even looking for. He'd never done this before, but then he'd never seriously thought he was mixing in those kinds of circles. Klemperer had mistaken him for someone from MI6, a ridiculous idea at the time, but here he was checking for bugs that might have been planted by his CIA paymasters.

He found nothing, but he waited until the search was complete before saying, "Are you hungry? Something to drink?"

They'd eaten on the train and she smiled, looking at her backpack as she said, "If you don't mind, I'll just crash—it's been a pretty long journey."

"Sure. You can sleep in my room, I'll sleep in the spare."

She looked a little puzzled and said, "You have a guest bedroom?"

He laughed, saying, "A spare room. I had a bed, then I got a new bed, so I put the old one in the spare room."

"Oh, okay." He thought she might suggest that they

could both sleep in his bedroom, but she didn't and he was surprised at how relieved he was. She was attractive and good company, and he wasn't sure if it was just the lack of an additional spark or, more likely, the fact that he wasn't ready, that he was still too afraid to open up, too afraid of intimacy and all that it might bring to the surface.

She kissed him on both cheeks and said, "Goodnight, Conrad. Tomorrow, we solve all your problems." He nodded, unsure how to respond, and she picked up her backpack and took it into his room, closing the door behind her and leaving him in the blank stillness of his own sitting room.

Conrad made himself some coffee and, once she'd settled, turned off the sitting room light and looked out into the street. A few days earlier, he'd looked out of the window and imagined himself under surveillance, a momentary flight of fancy after looking at Klemperer's disks. Now, after all he'd heard in the interim, it seemed just as fanciful to believe they weren't watching him.

Only the top floor of the building opposite allowed a view into his apartment, so he guessed if they were anywhere, it had to be there. Some of the windows were lit, people just visible inside, but he concentrated on the darkened ones, and had such a strong sense of the watchers beyond them that he had to move away from the window.

He glanced out casually a couple more times, but at least one apartment over there remained in darkness the whole evening. The thought of being seen, being watched, troubled him so much that he was tempted to go over there right now, but he held back, knowing how tired he was and sensing it might be best to let the dust settle before making a move.

In the end, he fell asleep on one of the sofas and woke up to a cold gray morning. He'd probably slept better than he would have done in the spare room anyway—he'd replaced that bed in the first place because it had given him a bad back.

He showered and dressed using clothes from his extra wardrobe in the spare room, ate breakfast, and left a note for Delphine, telling her that he'd be out for a couple of hours at most and not to answer the door for anyone. He was being overcautious, perhaps, but given what had happened to Gaddi and Fischer, he had no idea how cautious was cautious enough.

He went to the bank first and took Frank's SIM card from his box. Then he found a café he hadn't used before, inserted first Frank's, then Fox's SIM cards into his old phone and made a list of all the names and numbers in their address books.

There was no crossover at all in numbers, but then Fox had mentioned something about being off his usual patch. Fox's looked more like a personal phone, people's names attached to most of the numbers. There was certainly nothing to suggest its owner worked for the CIA, but then he supposed it wasn't something the agency's employees were likely to broadcast.

Frank on the other hand, ostensibly a civilian, had an address book that at first sight was almost as encrypted as his computer. All the names were down as initials only, but Conrad's numbers were listed under "DT." Frank had obviously used the final letters of each name instead of the initials. It seemed laughable, a piece of high theatre, and a code which wouldn't have taxed many of the people who might want to get their hands on Frank's phone in the first place.

There was "HR" for Friedrich Fischer, "OI" for Fabio Gaddi, "ST" for Julius Eberhardt. The two of possible interest to Conrad were "LD" and "MD," and given that he'd used Freddie's full name, he guessed the "MD" was the one he wanted—William Rutherford, the man Conrad guessed was either his Julius Eberhardt or, if he wasn't, would certainly know how to find him.

He took the SIM card out of the phone and slipped both cards back into his pocket. And he was still laughing to himself at the thought of Frank, squeezed into his too-young clothes, desperately trying to decode the initials every time he had an incoming call.

He wondered if Frank had really been no more "one of us" than Conrad had, and that the address book was all part of the make-believe that he was a trusted government agent and not just an unsavory conduit for dirty work. It was a scenario that fit with what he'd known about Frank himself, a man always desperate to fit in where he didn't belong. It made Conrad feel sorry for him, that he could have been so ill at ease in his own skin.

He walked back then, but called in at the building across the street from his. He'd seen the concierge a few times in the street, portly with thick gray hair and a red face, the kind of man who looked like he could drop dead at any minute but would probably make ninety without a hitch. He didn't appear to recognize Conrad, but then he guessed there was less to notice.

"Good morning. You speak English?" The concierge nodded but didn't seem inclined to try it out unless he had to. "I live across the road and I noticed one of the top floor apartments, the lights come on and off at strange times in the night, people coming and going—I thought you should know, in case there's something wrong up there."

The concierge shook his head dismissively and didn't look like he'd say anything at first, but finally said, "It's the Americans in the Mertens' apartment. It's only for one more week, that's what they tell me." Clearly then, they were pretty confident he wouldn't need to be watched for much longer, maybe for the same reason that a watch would no longer be required on Freddie's house, or Gaddi's.

In a neighborly way, Conrad said, "Typical. Americans!"

The concierge nodded agreement before saying acidly, "They're worse than the English."

Conrad smiled and left him to it, checking the number of the Mertens' apartment on the way out. He had the number of the man running the show and he'd confirmed that there were people watching him from across the street—not bad for a morning's work.

It was quiet in his own apartment and he assumed Delphine was in the bathroom or even still in bed. The first warning sign that something was wrong was the study, which had been turned over, not like a burglar would have done, but methodically.

He pushed open the bedroom door and that was the same. Her backpack was on the floor but barely visible underneath his own clothes, which had been emptied out of the wardrobe. The drawers had all been turned out, too. His instinct was to call out, but he didn't, because he knew she was either dead or gone and he didn't know if the people who'd done this were still in the apartment.

He took his gun out and threw the rucksack on the bed, checked the en suite bathroom, then moved through the apartment, expecting to find her at each turn. He hardly knew her, but he dreaded the thought that she'd been hurt, and at the same time, his deeply embedded cold streak was dreading the logistical nightmare that disposing of a body would entail.

He walked into the kitchen. His note was still on the table but she'd drawn a smiley on it. It made him smile, too, and saddened him, and made him realize that there would never have been anything between them, anyway.

Then, softly, almost unthreatening, a voice behind him said, "Put the gun on the table and turn around. If you try anything, I'll blow your head off."

He did as he was told. In nine years, he'd never once had a gun pulled on him, and now here he was with one pointing directly at his face, the biter bit.

Conrad Hirst

I met Jason on a bus in Egypt. It was a regular local bus, and we were the only two Westerners and got to talking. If I'm honest, I suffered him at first, thinking he wasn't the kind of person I wanted to be around—he seemed a little too enthusiastic, too much of a happy camper. But over the course of four hours on a bus, we never ran out of conversation.

To the extent that I ever had a best friend, he was it, and if it hadn't been for getting separated in Yugoslavia, I'm sure we'd still be close, best men at each other's weddings, godfathers to each other's children, you know the kind of thing. I do sometimes wonder, as I did the first time I saw one of his books, what we'd say to each other if we were to meet now, if it would ever be possible to fall back into the old routines. And in truth, I don't think it would, not anymore.

We ended up touring the Sinai together, then made the decision to head out to Thailand via India. We made other friends along the way, but we were a tight unit, and found ourselves always in agreement on whether we liked someone or not, whether to stay in a place or move on.

It was no surprise that we both tired of Thailand at the same time, nor that he knew I'd go for the idea of heading to Yugoslavia—to become the new Hemingway and Capa, as Jason liked to put it. I don't think he really believed I'd ever be a great photographer, and nor did I, but he certainly saw himself as the next Hemingway.

The point I'm getting to is that as much as we shared during that time, as close a friend as he became, I never told him about my parents. I never told anyone else either, not until I met you.

At first, with Jason, the subject simply hadn't arisen. We were near the end of the bus journey when he asked about college—he was a recent graduate and assumed I was, too—and when I told him I'd dropped out, he asked what my parents had thought of that. I told him they'd been fine about it.

I wasn't lying at that stage, I just thought it was too much baggage to dump into a conversation with someone I expected never to see again. And then I saw how much easier it was for them to be alive but distant—I didn't want people feeling sorry for me, for me to be the kid whose parents had died. I didn't want to have to talk about how I felt, or answer accusations that I was running away.

Of course, occasionally, I did lie, small lies—talking about them in the present tense, just to avoid suspicion. Strangely though, as time went on, it no longer seemed like lying at all. I'd talked about my parents so much, it was as if I'd resurrected them, and even I started to think of them as if they were still alive, still just a phone call or a letter away, content at home, occasionally worrying about their only son.

I never thought it odd, not until the day I told you, and then I realized that I'd been living a strange kind of denial. I'd lied for so long that, by the time I finally reminded myself of the truth, my memory of them was too distorted to grieve. In a different way, it was a trick I also played on myself when it came to losing you—and I suspect these letters are the closest I'll ever get to grieving properly.

The day I told you about my parents, I realized I'd slipped into a fictitious world, one in which they were still alive, and it astonished me that someone could so readily abandon reality, that my lies could have become a truth of their own. I know now, of course, that reality is a scarcer commodity than one might think.

I look back over the last nine years and I see that everyone I've met—except for the victims, if you could count those as meetings—has been a figment. It's a hard thing to take in, the realization that all the people you've dealt with have been playing parts and have been doing it for so long that the seams are no longer even visible. Even harder, perhaps, is the realization that I'm involved in the same show, and that I alone am ignorant of the part I'm meant to be playing.

Maybe this is just an exaggeration of every life—we all live in each other's fictions, both those created through lies and those born of misunderstanding. I could be fooling myself for thinking there's something else, but all the same, I want to be done with this. And the longer it drags on, the more confusing it becomes, the less concerned I am about how I take my exit.

Conrad

11

He was sitting on one of the kitchen chairs, hands cuffed in front of him. He'd put the cuffs on himself. Delphine stood in the doorway, maybe five or six feet away. She was holding the gun casually at her side now but she exuded the kind of confidence that suggested it wasn't worth making a lunge at her. Besides, he was intrigued.

"Where are the disks?" He looked questioningly, asking her to elaborate. "All I want is Klemperer's memoirs."

"Don't tell me, you're his publisher."

"You know when I said you were funny?"

"Point taken. Nevertheless, I don't have Klemperer's memoirs."

She smiled, self-satisfied, and was scathing as she said, "I was convinced you were faking. This whole business about not knowing you're with the CIA, I didn't believe anybody could be stupid or crazy enough for that to be true, but you are. I guess you're not stupid, so what is it? Did the nice little English boy get his head messed up in Yugoslavia? Is that your defense for being so gullible all these years, so mindless? You played at soldiers and couldn't handle it?"

"That's an interesting technique. Are you sure you're qualified for interrogations? I mean, what's next, embarrassing baby photos? Otherwise, maybe you could get to the point."

"The point is, we had Klemperer's house bugged. We know you have the duplicate disks."

"Who's we? French secret service? Swiss? Does Switzerland have a secret service?"

"That's not your concern."

He'd been trying to figure out how she was different, apart from the fact of holding him prisoner at gunpoint, and he finally realized that her charm seemed to have evaporated. He wondered if it had simply been part of her cover, and if that was why it hadn't quite worked on him.

"True. If I remember correctly, your bugs would have revealed Klemperer telling me to take the disks. Doesn't mean I took them. Like you said, I'm gullible, mindless, so why would I want the old man's memoirs? I'm not even a reader." She stared hard at him, sizing him up, but he decided to put her out of one lot of misery and into another. "As it happens, you're right, I did take them, but I was still telling you the truth when I told you I didn't have them. I picked them up from the bank this morning and posted them to Hoeffler."

"Interpol?" She looked angry and astonished. "You've got to be kidding me! Why would you do that?"

"Because he asked for them." He took some satisfaction from the crumbling of her composure. He thought back over the last couple of days, particularly the convincing act she'd put on in Freddie's house, and it felt good to be getting under her skin like this. "You know, you can despise me for it, but

I really am a simple man. Your acting skills might have been useful on someone like Frank Dillon, on anyone in your line of work, but if all you wanted was Klemperer's memoirs, you should have just asked me for them."

She swore under her breath in French and paced about for a few seconds, twitching with energy, her hand flexing around the gun. He wondered if she'd be in trouble for this, if it would be a black mark on her career, or if she simply believed in what she was doing and was upset at losing something she truly considered important.

Suddenly she became focused, pointing the gun at his face again as she said, "If you're lying to me, I swear . . ." She wouldn't shoot him—she wasn't behaving like someone who wanted to shoot anyone—but she was angry, maybe with herself as much as him, for what she perceived as a missed opportunity.

"Why would I lie, Delphine?" He was pretty sure now that her name wasn't Delphine and so, bizarrely, took some pleasure in using it. "Ask yourself, what on earth have I got to lie about? What have I got to protect?" Reluctantly, she lowered the gun again. "Why are you so desperate for the memoirs, anyway?"

She shook her head and said, "You're good at killing, I'll give you that. The way you killed Fox showed why you have a fearsome reputation . . ."

"I have a reputation?"

"In select circles," she said, a hint in her voice that it was nothing to be proud of. She didn't appear to understand that his only concern was the ever-receding horizon of anonymity, or, failing that, the alternate and riskier escape route that might lie in being widely known in this world. "But killing Fox also showed why you have no facility for intelligence work, because it was a stupid thing to do, counterproductive. What I'm telling you, Conrad, for your own good, is just forget Klemperer." She seemed subdued now, having accepted the loss of the disks and whatever consequences would follow, and as she deflated, some of the charm seemed to seep back into her.

"Okay, but just tell me one thing. Is that what this is all about? Fabio Gaddi disappearing, Freddie being killed . . . I take it you were never Freddie's girlfriend."

"Please, if his photograph was any indication!" She allowed herself a smile, momentarily looking as friendly as she had over the last couple of days. "I was convincing, wasn't I?"

"Oh yeah, I'll certainly hand you that."

"I don't know exactly what's happening with you. I think maybe it's a . . ." She searched for the correct word. "Would you say a convergence?"

"That sounds about right."

She nodded, as if saving the word to memory, and said, "Please don't move."

She walked away, her footsteps inaudible on the wooden floor. A convergence, he thought, and wondered whether his decision to quit had thrust him into the middle of things or saved him from the same fate as Freddie Fischer.

She appeared silently in the door again, her backpack slung over one shoulder, the gun still in her free hand. There was something else in that hand and she dropped it on the floor now, the key for the handcuffs. He offered an acknowledging nod of thanks.

"I did like you, Conrad—that wasn't an act. I think you

need help with your mind." He knew that to be true, but was still slightly hurt that she thought that way, or that it had been so obvious to her.

"That's why I'm quitting."

She looked uneasy, apparently in two minds whether to go or say something else, finally coming down on his side. "About that, the quitting. You need to go away, as far as possible, and a new identity. Do it now." Her voice was urgent. "I don't know why they're delaying, but they *will* kill you. It's how they work, eliminating all the risks. You can't bargain with them. Just go."

He looked her in the eyes and she held his gaze for a few seconds, reading his answer, before shaking her head in disbelief and walking away. He felt like calling after her, to make clear that he would go, that his defiant stare represented only a determination to go on his own terms, but she'd have probably considered even that suicidal.

As he sat there staring at the key on the kitchen floor, he realized she was right about one thing, that he didn't have the luxury of waiting for them to show their hand first. If he did, it would inevitably rob him of his chance to strike a blow for his own past. He was even confused about why it meant so much to him, but he couldn't just leave—deep in his core, he felt he had to go with the right blood on his hands.

Across the street, an American was keeping watch on his apartment. Maybe the time had come to pay him a visit, to see if he could start unraveling their operation and bring the rest of them out into the open. Everyone he'd met so far had treated him as someone to be reckoned with, even feared; now it was up to Conrad to make that fear tangible.

12

He closed the blinds and changed into a suit and overcoat from the new open-plan wardrobe Delphine had left him. He took a quick look in the mirror to reassure himself that he looked like a businessman, then headed down to the street.

Conscious that there could be someone keeping watch at ground level, he breezed straight across from his building to the other and walked past the concierge like he didn't exist. He could tell that the concierge had some vague recollection of him, but the suit and coat had done the trick and he went back to reading his paper without saying anything.

It was all about confidence, he realized that. For all these years, he thought he'd been good at killing people because of how detached he was, because he cared for nothing. But the real factor had been his absolute and unshakable confidence—he'd had so little at stake that the consequences of failure never troubled him, so the possibility of failure never registered.

Conrad took his gun out when he reached the Mertens' apartment, rang the bell, and held Fox's ID up to the spyhole. He heard someone approach the door and as soon as he heard the latch he stood back and gave it a kick, the door reverberating as it played percussion with the guy on the other side of it.

Conrad pushed with his hand, stepping into the gap. The guy was on the floor, wedged up against the wall. He could see directly through the hall to the sitting room where another guy was looking on in consternation.

He only needed one person. He slammed the door shut and shot the guy who'd answered it in the head. Conrad was already walking up the hallway as he fired the shot, avoiding the blood spatter. He aimed at the second guy as he walked toward him, quickly scanned the sitting room, and handed him the cuffs. He was pale and dark haired, gangly, and it was only up close that Conrad realized he was much shorter than he looked from a distance.

"Cuff yourself to the radiator." The guy fumbled badly as he put on the cuffs, shaking so much that Conrad thought he might have to do it for him.

He managed it on his own though, and once he was sitting on the floor, he said, "I'm unarmed, and there's no one else here."

Conrad could see the first assurance was true because he was wearing a blue shirt with a white T-shirt underneath, nothing in which he could have concealed a gun. "Give me your phone." The guy put his hand in his pocket and took out his phone, handing it up to him.

Conrad looked around the room. There was a whole bank of surveillance equipment, but nothing else. He looked through the rest of the apartment, which was entirely empty of furniture. The owners had clearly been away for some time. The kitchen had a microwave and a kettle, items of food here and there, but that was it.

He looked at the body in the hallway. The guy had slumped against the door, so Conrad grabbed his hand, one of the few parts of his body not sprayed with blood, and pulled him clear. The rest of the blood was sprayed or smeared on the walls and door, not so much on the floor. Not that he was too concerned about leaving evidence, because he doubted the local police would ever get to see this crime scene.

He walked back in to the prisoner. "Name?"

"Daniel Harrison."

"Why are you watching my apartment?"

Harrison looked panicked and said earnestly, "I don't know. I know you're Conrad Hirst, I know you're . . ." It seemed like he was about to give Conrad his job description but he changed his mind and said, "I know you're one of us. But I swear to God, I don't know why we're watching you. I was just told to keep an eye on the place, keep a record of your movements, any visitors."

"Where can I find Bill Rutherford?"

Harrison was having trouble keeping up with the briskness of the questions and, like Fox, his facial expressions were full of confusion. It was as if both men couldn't understand why Conrad was asking questions they seemed to think he should already have the answers for.

"I don't know whether he's in Luxembourg or not. He could be anywhere in Europe."

"Do you answer to him?"

"Yes."

"Where are you based?" Harrison shook his head, having reached the point beyond which he wasn't willing to an-swer questions. "The American Embassy?"

With a hint of panic, apparently fearful that it would be Conrad's next point of call, he said, "No! Jesus, no. Our sec-tion doesn't work out of embassies."

"So where?"

"Look, we're using a safe house. You know I can't tell you where."

Conrad shot him in the thigh. Harrison took the initial shock and pain of it through gritted teeth, but as he looked down at his leg and saw the blood immediately expanding across his pants, he started to breathe heavily, trembling, his composure scrambled. "Oh, God! Oh, God!"

Conrad looked at the wound. The blood wasn't pump-ing out, just spreading steadily, the cloth already sodden and heavy against his thigh. "It doesn't look like I hit the artery, which means the good news is you won't bleed to death in the next few minutes. But you will die unless someone sees to that wound."

"I can't tell you anything," Harrison shouted, his voice full of anger, once again as if these were things Conrad should have known and understood. He seemed to object more to Conrad's questions than to the fact that he'd shot him. "You know I can't tell you!"

Conrad nodded and pointed at the wound with the gun. "That'll be a slow death. Would you rather I did the decent thing?" He raised the gun and pointed it directly at Harri-son's head.

Surprisingly, Harrison actually calmed down and his tone was imploring but not seeking pity as he said, "I have a wife and two young daughters. Please, don't let me die. I know it means nothing to you, but I want to live."

What did he mean, that life in general meant nothing to Conrad, or merely Harrison's reasons for wanting to live? When Conrad thought about it, both were true anyway, and that was why he was angry with his life, why he wanted to change, because things that had once mattered to him more than anything were reduced now to intellectual curiosities.

He was shocked each time one of these agents implied he was a monster or out of control, but it was even more horrifying to realize they were right. How had he so completely blinded himself to the truth of what he'd become?

"I'll tell you what I'll do." He brought up the address book in Harrison's phone and handed it to him. "Select a number, any colleague who'll know where you are, who'll be able to get help."

Harrison looked suspicious, as if struggling to see what Conrad had in mind, perhaps wondering whether the pain and loss of energy were stopping him from thinking coherently and seeing the obvious. Finally, he scrolled through the list, laboring hard, and then handed the phone back to Conrad.

Conrad glanced down at the phone. "Good. I need fifteen minutes, maybe a little more. Then I'll call this number and tell them you're down. If you stay calm, try not to move, you'll have a pretty good chance of making it. That's the best deal I can offer today."

Harrison closed his eyes, nodding almost to himself, then opened them again and said, "Thank you."

"You're welcome," he said, and smiled, even though his good humor was lost on Harrison, because he was in pain and afraid, because he really didn't understand that Conrad had just pardoned him, nor that it was a first.

Conrad made his way back across to his own apartment.

It was a qualified risk leaving Harrison alive. He could have drawn them out just as easily with a phone call to announce Harrison's death, and in the unlikely event that Harrison was still conscious when they arrived, he could alert them to the fact that Conrad was after Rutherford.

But for all he knew, even that might not be a disaster. Just as an amateur could sometimes unnerve and beat a professional at chess, so his best asset was probably his unpredictability, the fact that his actions didn't always make sense. All he had to do was keep making his own decisions and keep pushing and, sooner or later, something would have to give.

He changed back into his regular clothes and loaded up his rucksack. He got his car and parked around the corner, then made the call, giving Harrison's colleague no time to respond before hanging up. He left the car where it was and made his way to the café along the street from his own building, a location that allowed him to cover the scene and still get back to the car if he needed to tail someone.

He sat in the window with a coffee and waited. He'd done a good thing in sparing Harrison—if he had spared him—a first faltering step back to what he imagined was normalcy. But he was eager to see who turned up here now, and as much as he was trying to set a fairer course for his life, he knew that Harrison would have to be the last person he spared today.

13

Conrad had only been in the café a few minutes when a car pulled up, braking hard. Two suited guys jumped out, one running into the apartment building, the other standing by the car and immediately making a call. Conrad heard the sirens then, and shortly afterward an ambulance appeared and the second guy ran inside with the crew.

A few of the other people in the café had been drawn to the window by the siren and were looking out now, waiting for something to happen. There were a few people standing in the leaden cold of the street, too, but there was a pretty quick turnover as people became bored by the lack of developments and the chill got to their bones. Even most of the people in the café gave up and went back to their tables.

Eventually, after about fifteen minutes, one of the suited guys came back to the car. It was the one who'd run in first, and he was visibly upset, perhaps for the struggling Harrison, perhaps for the dead man. Conrad tried to remember what the first guy had looked like, but could recall almost nothing about him, only the percussive thud of his body against the door.

He leaned against the car, but then looked into the lobby of the building and jumped to attention. The two paramedics wheeled Harrison out on a stretcher and answered a couple of questions from the concerned colleague as they loaded him into the ambulance.

The colleague waited until the ambulance had gone, its siren making clear that Harrison was still in danger. He looked ready to go back inside then, but stopped and looked along the street and waited. Conrad scanned the street and noticed a third man, this one in casual clothes, walking toward the building.

The two gave each other a handshake that turned into a comradely hug, then had a brisk but grave conversation. Conrad expected them both to go inside but, apparently happy that he was up to speed, the new arrival turned and walked back up the street, leaving the upset colleague to go into the lobby on his own.

Conrad left a tip and followed the guy walking up the street. At first he thought the guy might have left a car nearby, but he was on foot, which meant they had come from somewhere close by. He was smiling to himself as he followed, because even though this had been the whole idea of calling in Harrison's shooting, he couldn't believe they were making it this easy for him.

He walked quickly through the old town, then turned and headed down Montée du Grund. So their safe house was in Grund—an odd choice, he thought. He didn't know it well, but it was picturesque and lively, all huddled together down there in the river valley. If Freddie had lived in Luxembourg, it's where he would have found a house, but for some reason, he couldn't imagine these CIA drones feeling at ease in the place.

The guy he was following was on the phone now, the low burr of his voice occasionally sounding through the hollow winter air, though never loud or clear enough for Conrad to pick out words.

He was wearing beige chinos and a short dark overcoat scarily similar to the one Conrad was wearing. But he was confident that while his quarry looked like a CIA agent in civilian clothes, just as Fox had, Conrad didn't. He might have been stupid enough to become part of their operations, but despite what he kept hearing, he wasn't and would never be one of them.

Conrad followed him across the bridge over the Alzette and closed on him slightly as they walked into Grund itself. The guy took a right turn, then a left shortly afterward into a relatively quiet street. He picked up his pace and Conrad followed suit, passing parked cars, and too late he registered the car he'd just walked past and the doors opening behind him.

The guy ahead stopped suddenly and turned, his gun drawn, and Conrad didn't even need to turn himself to know that there was at least one person behind him. He stopped walking and held out his rucksack to the side. It was taken away from him by the guy behind, who spoke now in a drawling southern American accent.

"Let's take a ride, Mr. Hirst."

The guy he'd been following smiled when he got back to Conrad, and kept his gun on him as he dipped inside Conrad's coat, looking for a holster. He seemed grudgingly impressed when he found the gun nestled in the lining. He took a step back, gestured to his colleague for the rucksack and dropped the gun into it.

"You heard the man, get in the car. Our orders are not to hurt you, but after what you've done up there today, just give me an excuse. You hear me? Just give me an excuse." Conrad offered him an enigmatic smile but didn't speak, and he could see it rattled the guy just a little. "Turn around, slowly."

Conrad turned. The guy behind him and the other in the black Jeep they were driving were dressed like the first two to arrive on the scene for Harrison—suits, full-length overcoats. The Southerner got into the back with Conrad and kept his gun pressed so tight into his side that Conrad found himself looking out for potholes in the road, sensing that it would only take a small jolt for the Southerner to empty a bullet into him.

He was still coming to terms with having been so easily captured. He couldn't stand the thought that they'd read what he was doing and set him up from the start, although he had to admit now that his plan hadn't exactly been sophisticated. But he was convinced it had been more opportunistic than that, his quarry realizing he was being followed and calling it in, which would explain the phone call he'd made on the Montée du Grund.

He could imagine Delphine shaking her head disapprovingly, asking him if he'd learned nothing, asking him why he'd ignored her advice to go away. She was probably already on the way out of Luxembourg herself, having called in the bad news to her head office.

As grim as things looked though, Conrad would have had an answer for her, because he was at least where he wanted to be, heading into the center of their operations. If someone had asked him a week earlier to track down a CIA cell or section or whatever term they used to describe themselves, he wouldn't have known where to begin.

It wasn't far before the driver pulled up around the back of a house on the far side of Grund. He remained completely silent as they moved him from car to house and smiled at them whenever they made eye contact. It made them edgy but they kept it together as a fluid coordinated unit, covering him and each other without ever needing to talk or give instructions.

The house had apparently been rented furnished, with decent but utilitarian furniture throughout. His captors sat Conrad in a low armchair and the guy Conrad had been following said to the Southerner, "If he makes any attempt to get out of that chair, shoot him—I'll take full responsibility for it." He took out his phone then and made a call. "Sir, it's Hobson. We've got him in the safe house." Hobson listened, looking exasperated. "No, sir, we won't." The person on the other end obviously hung up without signing off because Hobson looked at the phone in irritation before closing it. The Southerner, who was sitting on the sofa now with his gun resting on his lap, looked at Hobson expectantly. Hobson said mockingly, "He'll be here in an hour—he's finishing lunch. Cooper's dead, Harrison's fighting for his life, thanks to this fucker, and *he* has to finish lunch."

The Southerner nodded and said, "I guess it's a business lunch of some kind. Hell, he probably has so many balls in the air he doesn't know what he's doing."

His conciliatory tone earned a derisive stare from Hobson, who collapsed into the armchair opposite Conrad and said, "May as well settle in. We could be waiting a while."

Conrad stared back at them. Hobson had probably been

blond as a kid and had the rugged, square-jawed looks of the all-around good guy, the college hero, the one who felt the biggest need for retribution when someone like Conrad started killing his colleagues.

The Southerner was blond even now but looked almost Asian, with high cheekbones and eyes so narrow they were hardly visible. At first sight there was something about him that made him look the meaner of the two, but he gave off an easygoing, almost gentle air.

"What do you want with me?"

It was the first time he'd spoken and the Southerner actually jumped. The driver had been in the kitchen but he walked in, as if wanting to know where the extra voice had come from. Even Hobson looked momentarily taken aback, but he regained his contempt and said, "You're the one doing all the killing, maybe you should tell us."

"I just want to see Rutherford."

"Yeah, well, you'll see him soon enough."

The Southerner, sensing that the ice had broken, sounded friendly but painfully puzzled as he said, "Why did you have to go and do that to Cooper and Harrison? I mean, we're all on the same side here. Why would you shoot them?"

Conrad turned toward him. "If we're all on the same side, why were they watching my apartment? If we're all on the same side, why did they send some guy called Fox from Berlin down to Lindau to follow me, and why did they kill Freddie Fischer?"

The Southerner looked questioningly at Hobson, who seemed to have the most authority in the room, and presumably most of the answers. He kept staring at Conrad as he answered his colleague. "He's just messing with your head.

Don't ask him any questions until Bill gets here, and don't listen to anything he has to say."

There was silence for a few seconds. The driver had been staring at Conrad in confusion since he'd come in from the kitchen, but he turned to Hobson now and said, "I thought he was one of us." Hobson looked questioningly, asking what his point was. "He's British. How can he be one of us?"

"Your friend has a point, Hobson. How can I be one of you? I'm the wrong nationality."

Hobson gave him a smug smile and said, "We're a complex organization, you know that, Hirst." He looked slyly vindictive, then added, "For what it's worth, you're the last existing component of what can only be described as a massive operational blunder, and I'll be happy if I'm the person who gets to close it down for good."

Conrad smiled, partly to get at Hobson, partly because he was finally beginning to get a sense of things. He guessed that at some point in the last ten years they'd decided to hire people in a blind capacity, people who would do any job, no questions asked, and who could never bring it back to the CIA's doorstep because they didn't even know that's who they were working for.

If that was it, Hobson was right about one thing, that it had been an operational blunder. Even without knowing whether there had been other recruits or what had happened to them, he could see that there were potentially disastrous risks involved. It was hard to believe the benefits could have been worth it, except of course that Conrad had done that job with cold efficiency until just three weeks ago.

"I'm taking a leak." It was the driver, speaking as he left the room. Hobson didn't take his eyes off Conrad, but immediately after the driver had left a phone began to ring. The Southerner patted his pocket, but it wasn't his. It was coming from Conrad's rucksack—he'd made a mistake, forgetting to turn it off or lose it, but he could see that slip working in his favor now.

"It's your friend Harrison's phone."

Hobson opened the rucksack and took the phone out. He looked at the number and stood up before answering, gesturing at the same time to the Southerner to keep an eye on Conrad.

"Daisy, hi, it's Jack Hobson. Has anyone contacted you?" He listened to the response and turned his back on Conrad, lowering his voice as he answered. "Now look, I don't want you to panic now. He's been shot in the leg, but he's in the hospital, he's being treated as we speak. Daisy, I don't know, but he's strong, he's a fighter. Look, I'm gonna call in right now, make sure there's someone on the way over to you. Okay, you take care now." He ended the call and took a deep breath, his shoulders heaving, as if overcome with a potent mixture of emotion and anger.

He put Harrison's phone in his pocket and opened his own phone again. Conrad assumed he'd just spoken to Harrison's wife, but he didn't have time to give it any thought. He heard the toilet flush, water rushing through the pipes, a tap being turned on. Hobson wasn't concentrating, and the Southerner was torn between looking at Conrad and wanting to ask Hobson about the phone call.

He didn't give himself time to think about it. The Southerner glanced at Hobson and Conrad sprang out of his seat, delivering a fierce punch to the back of Hobson's neck, and almost simultaneously bringing his right leg up to kick the Southerner in the head, a bruising kick that shuddered through the bones and muscles of his leg.

The Southerner went out cold, but Hobson was still on his feet. He'd stumbled forward and dropped his phone, but he was tough, fighting to recover himself. Conrad's rucksack was on the other armchair where Hobson had left it open and he dipped his hand into it now, pulling out his gun.

He could hear the driver on the stairs as he fired a shot into Hobson's back. It knocked Hobson forward and down, like he was diving into a pool, landing with a belly flop on the sitting-room floor. Conrad fired another shot into his head once he was down and turned sharply as the driver came into the room.

His footsteps on the stairs had obviously masked the noise of the silencer because he looked casual when he walked in, and it took him a moment to realize something was wrong. He saw Conrad first, then glanced rapidly around the room, Hobson dead and bloodied, the Southerner out cold. He considered going for his gun, but stopped himself before he'd done more than twitch his hand.

"Don't shoot," he said, holding his arms out. The Southerner moaned a little and stirred, his gun falling from his hand onto the floor. Conrad shot him in the chest, causing his body to jerk slightly. The driver jumped and said, "Oh, Jesus!" And Conrad recognized the look on his face, the look of a man who'd already accepted what was about to happen and was trying desperately to ready himself for it.

"Take your gun out, do it carefully, throw it over by Hobson."

The driver nodded and carried out his instructions, closing his eyes and breathing deeply. Conrad had thought the three of them were around his own age, but now that he looked at the driver, he guessed he was younger, maybe in his mid-twenties, probably still at the beginning of his career.

He had the look, that look they all seemed to have—a too-neat haircut; too-cleanly shaven; good American smiles. The only distinguishing feature about the driver was his eyes, which were startlingly blue, even more distinctive for being matched with dark hair.

"What's your name?"

He opened his eyes and looked at Conrad, the blueness of them almost unsettling. "Patrick de Vries."

Conrad nodded. "De Vries? That's a Dutch name."

"My dad was born in Holland." He swallowed hard and sounded dazed as he said, "Er . . . his parents brought him to America when he was two."

Conrad looked briefly again at the other two and then said, "I'm guessing we have an hour to wait. If you try anything in that hour, or if you do anything to warn Rutherford . . ."

"I understand," he said eagerly, as if cutting in before the threat was issued would help to ward it off indefinitely.

Conrad took the three discarded guns and dropped them into his rucksack, then took the phones from Hobson and the Southerner and turned them off. He stood back and gestured for de Vries to sit in the armchair with his back to the window. Conrad was cautious with him, but he could see from his body language that he wouldn't try anything, his decision no doubt influenced by the sight of his two senior colleagues.

Once de Vries had sat down, Conrad said, "If anyone calls you, answer it. If they ask where these two are, they went out to get groceries. You've got me covered, everything's fine. You get it?" He received a nod of acknowledgment. "If you give any warning, if you say anything that sounds remotely suspicious to me, I will kill you without hesitation."

De Vries nodded again and said, "I won't say a word."

"Will Rutherford come to the back or front of the house?"

"Front."

"Okay, so we wait."

De Vries looked across at the Southerner. He looked like he'd drunk himself into a stupor, like someone who might need to sleep for a couple of days, not like someone who'd never wake again. He could understand why it was rattling de Vries, because here was someone he knew, whose way of talking and turns of phrase were part of his everyday landscape, and he was both visibly there and irretrievably absent.

Conrad remembered when Lewis Jones had died. He'd been ill on and off for a couple of weeks, running a temperature, and then for a couple of days he'd been fine again. They'd been camped up in the woods, and Conrad and Jones had been sitting opposite each other, eating and talking. Afterward, Jones had fallen silent, like he was meditating, so Conrad had become quiet, too, and sat listening to the sounds of the autumn woods. It had taken one of the others to come over and realize Jones was dead, whether his heart had killed him or some virus. He'd turned forty-two earlier that same month.

They hadn't moved Jones and stood in a huddle some way off, discussing it with the commander, as if unsure what to do with the body or what had caused so sudden a death.

Maybe they'd also been discussing what they'd do with Conrad, as if responsibility for someone ill had passed to them with Jones's death.

Conrad saw most of this only in retrospect, but the Conrad who'd sat opposite his dead friend that day had known one thing as if it had been a sign, that the moment had come. He'd put his stuff together, slung it over his shoulder, and walked away.

A little way off, he'd stopped and looked back through the leaf-filtered light at Jones—still sitting upright, staring forever in Conrad's direction. Conrad had waved to him, knowing he was dead but still feeling it the right thing to do, as though he would see him in a few minutes. Then he'd turned for the last time and walked through those woods, down into the valley, and he'd kept walking until he'd left the war behind him.

At the time, through all of those months, it had seemed like he was living vicariously, watching himself from inside a locked room. Yet now he could remember some of it—like the day with Jones in the woods—as if it had happened earlier that morning, as if Jones were still sitting there, thinking, ready to expound his garbled philosophy of life.

Despite everything, nearly all his memories of Jones were good ones. The only cloud was that Jones had told him about Frank Dillon, had told him that if ever he was stuck, he could go to Mittenwald and tell Frank that Lewis Jones had sent him. But even in that, he could no more blame Jones for the things he'd done than he could have blamed Anneke.

De Vries tried to speak but had to clear his throat first before saying, "Why didn't you kill me?"

"I need you alive." He didn't finish the sentence—for

now—knowing de Vries would be less likely to try anything if he thought Conrad intended to spare him.

"Why did you . . . ?" He ground to a halt, looking at the Southerner.

"Because I only need one of you alive and I couldn't keep more than one of you under control." For some reason he once again objected to the sense he'd gotten from these people that he was the bad guy, not because of the sentiment but because it was coming from them. It was true, he'd killed for money in the belief that it was on the behest of a criminal gang, but in the light of the emerging facts, he thought he'd acted with considerable restraint over the last few days. "Look, I've been killing people for this agency for nine years, most of them probably innocent, just people who were inconvenient or political irritants—I don't know, but you people are in no position to get precious about me killing some of your own. And another thing, I gave Harrison the chance to live. I could've killed him, I should've. Hard as it might be for you to understand, shooting Harrison in the leg is the nicest thing I've done in the last decade."

De Vries looked taken aback by Conrad's final statement, but quickly regained his composure and said, "So why did you?"

"What?"

"Why did you give him a chance?" From the way he was asking questions, from his open-minded tone, Conrad got the impression de Vries was one of the few who hadn't seen his file, and was genuinely interested in finding out who Conrad was.

"Honestly? I did it because I thought it was the right thing to do. I didn't know it was right, I didn't feel it, I just suspected. And I'll tell you something else, I'm pissed off for not knowing, for even having to think what the right thing might be. I wasn't always this person."

"So what happened?"

He liked this guy, de Vries, he was personable, but he drew the line at giving that much of himself, even if he could rightly sum it up in a few sentences. Besides, he knew he'd only end up sounding like he was trying to justify himself, and there was no justification—even if he'd been sick, he'd allowed himself to fall sick, and had betrayed Anneke in the process.

"I don't want to talk anymore."

De Vries shrugged acceptance, but then said, "Thanks, anyway." Conrad looked at him questioningly. "For not killing Harrison. He's a good guy."

Conrad didn't respond and they fell into silence. De Vries seemed happy enough to sit like that, as if he were waiting for a train or plane. Conrad was content, too, and having thought about it once, he kept thinking back to Jones sitting in the autumn light in the woods that day many years ago.

He had no idea where it had been, just as he had no idea how far he'd walked or through what dangers. Somewhere along the way, he'd flagged down an antiquated bus, the driver and passengers visibly relieved that he was on his own and only wanting a ride. He'd spent a couple of hours on that bus, and once on their way, a couple of the passengers had offered him food and drink, making him aware of how their view of him had shifted from threat to protector.

There had been another bus north after that, and in a small town he'd given his weapons and ammunition to a young guy with a vintage rifle and makeshift uniform. By the time he'd boarded a train to Innsbruck he'd become a civilian again, and if he'd headed west instead of north, back to England rather than into Germany, he'd have remained that way.

He didn't know why it was occupying his thoughts so much, except perhaps that he was on a parallel journey now, through uncertain terrain, its outcome determined by the smallest decisions. And even though he was focusing his attention on Rutherford, if indeed Rutherford was his Eberhardt, he realized that killing him would give him no assurances for the future, merely the satisfaction of drawing a line under the past.

De Vries seemed to hear the car first, cocking his head to one side. A couple of seconds later, a black Mercedes pulled up outside. Conrad got up and stepped across Hobson's body. He stood to the side of the window, and stared out at the car through the haze of the net curtains.

A guy got out of the back of the car on the far side, and Conrad recognized him instantly. Just as he'd hoped, it was the man who'd been introduced to him nine years ago as Eberhardt. He was hardly changed, only a little more gray in his hair. So Fox had indirectly told him yet another thing that was useful, that this man was Bill Rutherford. It seemed if ever a man had deserved to live, it had been Fox.

Rutherford looked at the house over the top of the car and Conrad sensed immediately from his calculating expression that he wouldn't come in, that he knew something was wrong. He took out his phone and pressed a couple of buttons before putting it to his ear. He was calling Hobson, he had to be, because moments later he jumped back into the car and it sped off, screeching up the street.

It had been worth a shot, but he was frustrated that they'd waited for nothing, that the guy's antennae were so finely tuned. He also knew that time would now be short, that Rutherford would be calling for back-up to take the house. He stepped back over Hobson and pointed his gun at de Vries, who looked alarmed by the development and unsure of what could have brought it about.

"Where's he staying?" De Vries swallowed hard, the look of a man desperate to find some middle ground, all the while knowing it didn't exist. "Simple choice, talk or die—where is he staying?"

"The Holstein International in Kirchberg."

"Room number?"

"622." Conrad nodded, but de Vries seemed to see through him and immediately shook his head, as if annoyed with himself for being so gullible. "You lied. You're gonna kill me, aren't you?" He didn't appear afraid, just angry, as if he'd taken Conrad at face value, giving him the benefit of the doubt over the death of his colleagues, and now felt betrayed.

"I have no alternative," said Conrad, feeling he at least deserved an explanation. "Rutherford could already be spooked enough to change hotels, but he certainly will if you tell him I know where he is."

"So tie me up, knock me out, leave me here. What was all that stuff about doing the right thing?"

"An ideal, one I don't have time for right now. Rutherford's probably already called the cavalry—I'd say I have five, ten minutes at most."

De Vries looked defiant as he said, "I won't beg, I won't die pleading, but you don't have to do this. You might lie to yourself, tell yourself you have no choice, but you don't have to kill me."

Conrad admired the guy's guts and dignity, and if there had been another way, he'd have let him live, but he couldn't take him along and he couldn't leave him to talk because either would place one more obstacle between him and Rutherford. And that's what this had all finally boiled down to, Conrad and Rutherford.

"Yes, I do." He took aim at his head, knowing that this was a death he'd regret, and even taking some comfort in that cold thought.

Conrad Hirst

Dear Anneke,

It's nearly done. I wish I could say I've acted well over these past days, in a way that you would have understood or found forgivable, that wouldn't have horrified you. But I've come a long way from being the boy you knew, and if it's even possible, it will be a much longer journey back.

I've already killed more people than I set out to kill, but I swear I have only one more death to deliver, that of Bill Rutherford, the man I knew as Julius Eberhardt.

I can't even tell you with any clarity why I've come to focus with such determination on him, but I have, and you see, I don't have time to stop and consider reasons, to make sense of things. I have no more time to think than you did that day in the market square. The world is in flux around me and I have to act or be swept away. I have to kill Rutherford. I know it even if I don't understand it.

It already seems a distant age when I stared at the real Eberhardt on the chapel steps in Birkenstein, the landscape softened white with snow. He looked down at me and would probably never have guessed that I had once worked for him.

I did work for him to begin with, I'm certain of that, those early jobs with Schmidt, the last of which was the drug dealer in Stuttgart. I can't even remember what he'd done wrong, whether he was selling drugs on Eberhardt's turf or skimming profits. Whatever it was, we were sent to put pressure on him, or Schmidt was. I was little more than a body in a suit at that point, there to make up the numbers, to intimidate on cue with a little gentle violence.

The dealer lived in a top-floor apartment in a five-story building. And I remember how alarmed I was by the sight of him. The guy was in his thirties, which seemed old to me at the time, but he was wearing striped spandex leggings and a black vest, long black hair, a skin-cancer tan, like a throwback to some hackneyed metal band from the '80s.

He looked ridiculous but he was defiant, snapping back at Schmidt, snarling at him. Of course, they were speaking in German so I had no idea what they were talking about. I just stood there looking on, disinterested. Then Schmidt turned to me and said, "Maybe he needs to go over the balcony." The wink was what I missed, the intimation that we would show this guy how scary we were without actually being scary.

So I threw him over the balcony. I walked fast toward him, pushed him and kept pushing him, so quickly, so fiercely, that he never had time to dig his heels in or take hold of anything. He yelled some panicky questions over my shoulder to Schmidt, but that was it. I heard something in his body crack as he hit the railing at the top of the balcony, but he went over with such momentum that it would have been hard to stop him.

He didn't die straight away. He lay down there screaming in the parking lot, but by the time we left and a small crowd had gathered, he was silent. A woman, I'll always remember how decent she looked, like someone's loving mother, spat on him where he lay on the ground.

Schmidt panicked. He told me Eberhardt would be furious, though I can't say it concerned me. I had nothing to fear from Eberhardt or anyone else. At that precise point in time, there was nothing left in me, nothing that could be hurt. I thought I had no farther to fall, but I was wrong, and reached the bottom more recently than I'd like to admit, even to myself.

I think I've told you once before how they found me, sitting in my room in Die Alpenrose, staring up at the lonely light of the cable car station, taking comfort from it. You know, I never actually took that cable car ride—I didn't need to. What mattered to me was that the station was always up there on the mountain, the light always shining.

Frank introduced me to Eberhardt. He had a very slight German accent, and only now do I know that even that hint of an accent was faked. He was an American and I was being recruited to work for the CIA. I'm tempted, when I look back on the person I was then, to say they were crazy, but in one sense they knew exactly what they were doing, because for nine years I did their bidding without question.

I was damaged and cold and pliable, I killed without ever wondering why I killed or who these people were, what they'd done. I talked to no one, had no friends, I lived and killed in a vacuum. If I hadn't gone to Chur, I would have continued to kill for them.

I wish I hadn't had to kill Klemperer. I wish it more as the weeks go on. But indirectly, I'm grateful for that job because it brought me to this point, and in one way or another, it made me fully understand what I've lost, and perhaps what's still within my power to regain.

I only wish that included you. I'd kill a hundred Eberhardts or spare a hundred Rutherfords if I thought it could ever bring you back. But you and I, we existed for only a moment, and then both disappeared forever.

I love you,
Conrad

14

He studied the hotel from across the road. It was called The Metropolitan, and he could imagine a lot of people turning up and being disappointed. It was low-rent and in the modern quarter, the kind of place where they wouldn't ask questions for one night.

Conrad pulled around the corner and parked the car on the side of the street, then turned and said, "It's a small hotel, probably one person in the lobby, maybe a couple of passing guests. If you try anything, you have to know that I'll kill them as well as you—I'll have no choice."

De Vries nodded. "I won't try anything."

"Good, let's go."

He didn't know if de Vries was a man of his word or if he simply appreciated how lucky he was to still be alive, but he got the feeling he could trust him to play the game. And, of course, de Vries also knew that Conrad was carrying a gun in his coat and that he would shoot as many civilians as it took to ensure there were no witnesses.

It had been bone cold the whole day, but a wind had

picked up now and brought a little sleet with it. De Vries huddled against its sting and hurried so that he was a step ahead of Conrad going into the lobby, if lobby was the right word for it—a narrow hallway with a desk on one side, a couple of upright chairs, a dim light.

A bored-looking woman came out from a back room. She had the look of someone who lived there and could no longer be bothered to present herself to the outside world— the clothes and hair all giving the impression of someone slopping around at home on a Sunday morning.

"A twin room, please. One night."

"You have a reservation?" Conrad shook his head, but it hardly seemed to matter. She picked a key apparently at random off the board, suggesting the hotel was close to being empty.

Despite the first impressions, the room was surprisingly clean, even fresh. De Vries took his coat off and threw it on one of the beds. Conrad moved a small table next to the armchair in the corner of the room, put his gun on the table, the rucksack next to it, then threw his own coat on the other bed before sitting in the chair.

Conrad had a view of the door from there and was just to the side of the window, which meant he could look out but wasn't in range of a sniper if they did somehow manage to track him down. He wasn't convinced they had those kinds of capabilities, but he didn't want to lapse into complacency—he'd come too far.

He knew he'd already taken a risk by letting de Vries live. It had slowed him down for one thing, forcing him to put off Rutherford for another day. And that meant they had to spend the night here, with Conrad knowing that every hour of inactivity on his part would be matched by an hour of frantic search and preparation by Rutherford and his people.

The only positive aspect of the delay was that he'd give them a chance to settle down. Getting to Rutherford that afternoon, after he'd sped away from the safe house, might well have been impossible anyway. By leaving it till morning, he might allow them to develop a little complacency of their own.

De Vries was still standing, looking around the room, so Conrad said, "Why don't you sit down? We have a long wait ahead of us."

He nodded and then went through a strange routine, taking his shoes off, his jacket and tie, then putting his overcoat back on and sitting on the bed, pulling the overcoat around him like a blanket. Conrad didn't think it was cold in the room.

De Vries didn't say anything for a while, but finally he looked over at Conrad and said, "What's your Dutch connection?"

"What do you mean?"

"When you asked about my name being Dutch, it seemed to have some significance."

Conrad shook his head. "Not really. I had a Dutch girlfriend a long time ago, that's all."

"What happened?"

Was it that obvious just from his tone? Whether or not, he didn't want to get into that conversation, certainly not with de Vries. He'd let him live, he liked him, but he didn't see them becoming friends. And he could hardly forget that, as compliant as de Vries had been, he'd seen Conrad kill his colleagues and it was his duty still to stop him.

"Nothing happened."

"But you're not together anymore?"

"I told you, it was a long time ago," said Conrad, trying to sound casual, implying de Vries was reading too much into a couple of throwaway comments.

De Vries fell silent again, but a few minutes later he said, "What will you do tomorrow?"

Conrad thought ahead, saying, "I'll go to Rutherford's hotel and kill him, or at least, that's the plan. After that, I don't know. It's up to them, I suppose. I'll have done what I set out to do."

"You think they'll let you go?" For de Vries and everyone else, it was probably the obvious question, pointing as it did to the biggest flaw in his plan. He guessed they were trained in strategic planning and it was beyond their comprehension to see someone like Conrad, running headlong toward what could only be a Pyrrhic victory by their standards.

"You're the CIA man, what do you think?"

"I don't know," he said, though it was clear what de Vries really thought, that Conrad was already a dead man and had been for some time. He came close to admitting as much when he said, "You know, you could still make a run for it, disappear. Despite what you might think, we don't have unlimited resources. I couldn't imagine them worrying too much about tracking you down."

"Even after what's happened here?"

Conrad thought the mention of the three agents he'd killed today would hit de Vries, reminding him whose side he was on, but he persisted, saying, "Particularly after what's happened here. The prospect of losing a few more agents just to dig you out of some hole in Asia or South America, that's not something they'll want to justify."

He was right about them all thinking alike, with de Vries making the same argument that Delphine had made to him, and he imagined neither had made it out of any ulterior motive, but rather because it was what they'd have done themselves in the same situation.

"Maybe I'll do that. But not until I kill Rutherford."

"Getting Bill really means that much to you?" Conrad stared at him, the answer hardly needing to be voiced. "But that's what I don't get. You were part of his op, you worked for him for nine years, got paid well. Why now?"

"You don't know anything about this, do you?" He remembered him being surprised back at the house when Conrad had spoken in an English accent, and his subsequent questions. "In fact, you're quite possibly the only person who knows less than me."

"Don't count on it. Your op with Rutherford is so secret, most of us don't even know what it's called. I think Hobson knew, but I was never told. All we were told was that there's a rogue agent, part of a highly classified operation, now working for persons unknown, killing all his old contacts."

For the briefest moment, Conrad had been optimistic, hearing how few people knew about him and the operation he'd been duped into being a part of. It made him think there was still an escape, still a chance to achieve his original objective of shutting down all the channels to his past.

But listening to the cover story that had been fed to de Vries and the others, Conrad realized he was up against the lumbering and unstoppable mechanics of a global organization. They'd been clever, too, using aspects of the truth to thread authenticity into the lie they'd created for him.

And he could see now that there was no hope, either, in

being on the radar of Interpol or countless other organizations. He could imagine how neatly embroidered the cover story would be, and how no one would question the manner in which the CIA cleaned up its own mess.

"I was in Yugoslavia, fighting as a mercenary."

De Vries sat up and said, "You were a mercenary?"

"I became one out there—it's a long story. Anyway, I was fighting for nine months, a year maybe, and when I got out I'd been told a guy called Frank Dillon would find me work. He did, acting as, I don't know, an enforcer I suppose, for a German crime boss. I killed somebody, and they'd clearly been watching me, knew how messed up I was, and Frank and the crime boss paid me a visit and told me they could use a man like me."

"As in . . . ?" It was as if he knew the answer but wanted confirmation.

"As in, willing to kill without question, I suppose. There was a lot of talk about discretion, but I presume I just ticked all their boxes. I was a blank canvas."

"So they could paint you any way they wanted," suggested de Vries, running a little too far with the metaphor.

Conrad smiled and said, "I think you're missing the point. They didn't want to paint me at all, they wanted me to remain void—that was the exact quality they wanted." De Vries looked deep in thought, as if he couldn't take in all he was hearing, either about his own agency or the way it had treated Conrad. "So that's how I became a hitman. And I've only found out in the last few days, only by trying to get out, that I never did meet that crime boss. The person I met was Bill Rutherford, I knew it for certain only this afternoon, and I changed employers the night I met him. I was twenty-three."

De Vries leaned back against the headboard again, looking astonished. Conrad wondered if it was because he'd mentioned his age, maybe a couple of years younger than de Vries was now. It astonished Conrad himself now that he'd said it, to think that after such a comfortable upbringing he could have become so rotten so young.

It was a blessing his parents were dead, that they hadn't had to see him like that. But then, if they hadn't died he'd have stayed at college and would have existed in a parallel universe, one in which he'd never gone to Yugoslavia, never met Anneke—the memories crashed into each other, happy and sad, all equally intangible.

De Vries seemed to be working through something in his thoughts, and after a minute or so, he said, "I don't get it. I understand you're pissed because you were lied to, even exploited, but you thought you were killing for a criminal. Surely it should come as a relief to discover that you were killing for the government, hitting legitimate targets." Korn had said the same thing, and it almost made Conrad wonder if he was missing some glaring truth.

"People keep saying that. But if my targets were legitimate, why were they using me?" De Vries didn't answer and, thinking aloud, Conrad said, "I was sick, in the head, maybe I still am. They knew I was sick and they employed me because of it. Ask yourself what kind of person or organization takes advantage of a broken twenty-three-year-old like that? I set out to kill the crime boss for it, but I can at least understand his lack of scruples, his moral emptiness. I'm not naïve, I know what governments are like, but it still fills me with rage to know that someone in Rutherford's position could use his power like that."

He was concerned he'd come across as self-pitying, blaming everyone but himself, which wasn't how this had all started. But de Vries nodded anyway, and looked sad and reflective. "You're right, we shouldn't operate like that." He paused before adding earnestly, "I'm nobody, but as a representative of the CIA, I'd like to be the first to offer you an apology."

Conrad laughed and said, "Apology accepted." De Vries smiled, then he also laughed. "But I'm still killing Rutherford."

"I know." He laughed again, perhaps at the fact that he was idly agreeing to the death of his own boss. Even so, Conrad still had to assume de Vries would try to stop him, so he wouldn't let some shared laughter trick him into thinking they were now on the same side. "Do you mind if I eat?"

"Go ahead."

Conrad had allowed him to fill an overnight bag with food and drink from the kitchen of the safe house, and he watched now as de Vries opened the bag and emptied the contents onto the small dressing table. He offered Conrad a plastic bottle of Coke, which he took, then some food, which he declined. De Vries put a few things together, cradled them in his arm and went back to the bed.

He sat cross-legged as he ate and it made him look like a student somehow. Maybe if he'd stared at any of the others long enough, he'd have begun to get a sense of a personality in each of them, too, but de Vries seemed more real than the others.

Conrad could imagine him having been a student, growing up somewhere, having friends who weren't part of the agency. Possibly de Vries was different, or possibly he just hadn't been in long enough for the edges to be worn smooth.

"Tell me about yourself, Patrick."

Awkwardly, through a mouthful of food, he said, "What do you mean?"

"I mean, where did you grow up, go to college? Do you have a girlfriend? Is this what you always wanted to do?"

De Vries obligingly took a swig of Coke and hurried to finish what was in his mouth. "Grew up in Boulder, Colorado, went to Brown, which is . . ."

"Brown? Which is what?"

De Vries betrayed the slightest flicker of surprise that Conrad didn't know, but said, "It's an Ivy League university, in Providence, Rhode Island. And it was there that I decided I wanted to work for the government. As for the girlfriend, technically, yeah, but she's in London, which is where I was until a month ago, and now I don't know where I'm gonna be from one week to the next, so I don't know how it'll work out."

Conrad thought of the girlfriend in London and wondered how her life would have changed if he'd killed de Vries earlier that day. If they were drifting apart, maybe she'd have been upset, devastated initially, but also just a little relieved, and then guilty for feeling like that. Otherwise, it would have been a wound she'd have carried through her whole life, every memory of de Vries rendered bittersweet.

"So you skied a lot, as a kid?"

"Every winter sport imaginable. I love going home in winter even now." He smiled to himself as if thinking of being there. "What about you?"

"Yeah, we took a skiing holiday every year, but I think you have to live in the mountains to get really good."

"No, I meant, where did you grow up and stuff?"

"Oh. Dorset, it's a small county . . ."

"No, I know it, kind of next to Devon, right? It's beautiful."

"Yeah. Went to university in York, but I dropped out. My, er, my parents were killed in a car crash."

"I'm sorry," said de Vries, looking truly saddened, even after everything he'd heard or witnessed today. Maybe de Vries loved his parents more than Conrad had loved his, because as the years had gone by, he'd always been slightly ashamed of himself at how easily he'd gotten along without them.

"Yeah, they were on their way to the airport, to go skiing as it happens. Next thing I knew, I had lots of money and no more parental expectations." De Vries shook his head and looked at the food in his hand, as if he thought it might be in bad taste to carry on eating. "But please, Patrick, I don't want you thinking that's why I ended up the way I did. After my parents died, I came closer to having a happy life than I ever could have hoped for—it just didn't turn out that way."

"Still, it must have knocked you sideways." Conrad nodded, but felt a small pang of guilt, knowing his reaction, his grief, had been nothing compared to what he'd felt for Anneke. "Do you get back to England much?"

Conrad shrugged and said, "Haven't been back in twelve years. No reason to go back—I don't have any other family there. If I went back now, I don't even know where I'd go. I'd feel like a tourist." He felt exposed now, having said too much about himself, and shifted the conversation back to de Vries. "So, anyway, has your family always lived in Boulder?"

"Not my dad, obviously—he grew up in Pennsylvania, but my mom grew up in Colorado."

Conrad continued to ask him questions, though de Vries didn't need much encouragement to talk about his family and friends and hometown. And as Conrad listened to him talking about these things, not as something locked away in the past, but as a current part of his life, he had an acute sense of what he had come close to destroying earlier that day when he'd considered killing him, not just the boyfriend of a girl in London, but someone who was cherished.

Thousands of miles away, de Vries was part of a little world which would have been shattered by his death. He knew the same could probably be said of many of the other lives he'd ended, but Conrad couldn't allow himself the space to think of those people. It was enough to feel an underlying sense of relief for having let de Vries live. It was a start.

Perhaps the most natural reaction would have been to compare his own life to the richness of the life de Vries was describing, but that didn't occur to him. Conrad had no family to go back to, no friends to share his hopes or plans for the future with, no place where he belonged, no world that would be torn asunder by his death, yet somehow he'd never thought of these negatives as being part of his problem.

It was only later that evening, with de Vries sleeping under his overcoat rather than in the bed, the lights out in the main room, that Conrad looked out the window onto the cold and rain-disheveled city and realized it wouldn't be enough to just quit. His life had become so stripped down, so devoid of human contact, it was as if he were emerging from ten years in solitary confinement.

And it scared him. He'd strayed so far from the way most people lived that he didn't know how to begin. There were no real friendships to rekindle, and Conrad didn't know how people went about making new friends. Nor did he know how people of his age went about finding girlfriends, and even if he were able to, how would he explain the strange emptiness of his life?

He'd thought the biggest obstacle to building a new life would be his private history of death, the years for which he could offer no biography. Yet much worse was that he knew nothing of how people led their lives.

He'd once been a social person, a person confident enough to capture the heart of a woman as beautiful as Anneke, and now even he hardly noticed his own presence in a room. It was as if he'd been bled slowly over the years until he'd faded to nothing.

Suddenly, he couldn't stand to dwell anymore. He sat down in the armchair and tried to think of nothing, and catnapped on and off through the night. At one point, he was wakened by de Vries getting up and going to the bathroom. He watched under lowered eyes to make sure he didn't try anything, but de Vries looked over at him when he came out, then simply climbed back under his coat.

Conrad didn't wake properly until it was light and was surprised when he saw that it had turned eight. The rain and sleet had long since stopped, but the sky was low and leaden and clinging like mist to the tops of the buildings. It probably wouldn't get much lighter in the next couple of hours.

He put his gun in his coat and took his rucksack into the bathroom with him, and when he came out, de Vries had stirred and was sitting up on the bed, swigging the remains of a bottle of Coke. He looked over at Conrad and said sleepily, "Hey, morning."

Conrad stared back at him, thrown by the unfamiliar little intimacies of friendship, and said, "Yeah, look, I need to tie you up with something." De Vries looked puzzled. "I have to leave you here, I have to make sure you can't alert Rutherford. Even if I could trust you, you'd find it pretty hard to explain if you're not tied up when they find you."

"I didn't think of that." He looked around the room, then said, "What about the cord from the drapes?"

Conrad looked over at the curtains, which opened and closed with a cord pulley system. He took the knife from his rucksack, cut the cord loose, then cut it in two.

De Vries stood up and said, "Let me go pee first." He went into the bathroom and once he'd finished, leaned back out. "This could be a good place. You can tie me to the towel rail."

Conrad followed him into the bathroom and found him kneeling with his back to the heated towel rail with his hands up. Conrad felt the rail, cold, then pulled at it to see how strongly fixed it was. He tied de Vries's hands to the rail, then took a step back and looked, making sure he hadn't missed anything, making sure de Vries wasn't taking him for a ride.

"You should gag me, too."

"Of course." Conrad took a pillow case and ripped it open, but curiosity won the day before he put it on. "Why are you being so helpful?"

De Vries smiled, open and friendly as he said, "Isn't it obvious?" Conrad shook his head. "Because I believe you, and because you saved my life. You had no reason to spare me but you did. I'll never forget that."

"Okay," said Conrad, once more made uncomfortable, this time by his gratitude. "Look, if I have a chance, I'll tell someone where you are. If not, the room's only booked for one night, so someone's bound to come in a couple of hours from now, a maid or someone. You'll be okay till then."

He made to take a step forward, but de Vries said, "Conrad . . ." It was the first time he'd used his Christian name, and the familiarity caught Conrad off guard. "You know, you could still walk away. I know you wanna kill Rutherford, but if you do kill him, they'll think you're not gonna stop, and they'll come after you. Trust me, if you kill Rutherford, they *will* kill you. Walk away now—it's not worth it."

Conrad smiled and said, "You don't get it, do you, Patrick? You're weighing my satisfaction in killing Rutherford against the loss of a life like yours. There's nothing at stake here, nothing at all."

De Vries didn't argue, but said only, "Well, good luck, anyway."

"Thanks." He wound the gag around, pulling it tight into his open mouth. He was about to leave but asked finally, "Does the Jeep have a tracking device?" De Vries shook his head and Conrad left.

He realized there was nothing rational in his determination to kill Rutherford. He hadn't known who the man was until a couple of days before, and his original plan to kill four men had been about making a clean break, not a desire for revenge.

And revenge wasn't even an appropriate response, because these people had merely taken advantage of the person he'd already become. Maybe Conrad had become so focused on killing Rutherford because he represented that part of himself, the part he wished to eradicate. Maybe he just felt the need to kill someone important enough to make a difference.

If it worked, if he drew a line in the sand, he'd have plenty of time to think through his reasons, to place them in the context of the mess that was his adult life. And if de Vries was right, then Conrad would be out of it and it would be left to someone in the CIA to ponder his motives.

Perhaps de Vries would be among those asked to write a report, part of an attempt to assess the state of Conrad's mind. If that was how it ended, if that report came to be written, Conrad was only sorry he wouldn't be around to read it himself.

15

The Holstein International was an expensive but anonymous place, glass and steel and drab concrete, probably built in the 1980s. It could easily have been the headquarters of a corporation like the institutional buildings that surrounded it, and even the open expanse of lobby did little to differentiate it. Conrad imagined that was what made the people staying there feel comfortable.

He was walking toward the main doors and looking in through the plate glass at the brightly lit interior when he spotted a familiar face. There were a couple of guys in suits, sitting in low leather chairs, positioned so that they could see everyone coming into the hotel. Nothing marked them out from the other people in the lobby, but one of them was the guy who'd been upset by the scene in the Mertens' apartment.

The agent wasn't looking in Conrad's direction, so he turned casually and headed around the side of the hotel, through a service gate and around to the back. There were plenty of cameras about and if Rutherford's people had access to them Conrad probably wouldn't have much of a window. He huddled against the cold and kept his head down as much as he could without looking suspicious, but he knew there was a slim chance they'd have him marked before he got inside.

He followed the smell of food, walked through a couple of sets of swing doors, and found himself surrounded by the clamor of the kitchen. A few of the chefs and kitchen assistants immediately stopped what they were doing and stared at him.

Conrad flashed Fox's ID at them and they looked disgruntled but went back to work. One, a bulky, red-faced chef, stared for a little longer, as if trying to control his anger. It gave Conrad the impression that the hotel staff had seen more than enough American security personnel over the previous days and were getting sick of the intrusion.

He played his part, walking through the kitchen as if checking it out for his own benefit, then strolling casually into some kind of service corridor. He headed for the elevator, but as he stepped into it, a guy in a dark suit appeared from a doorway further up the corridor and shouted, "Hey, hold the elevator!"

He was American, quite possibly one of Rutherford's men, and Conrad only had a second to make a decision. There was a chance he'd get there before the doors closed anyway, and if he didn't he might become suspicious that Conrad hadn't held them for him.

He took the risk, holding the doors open until the smiling American joined him in the elevator with a genial, "Thanks, buddy." He could have been CIA but could just as easily have come from across the narrow divide and been a Mormon missionary, though Conrad guessed the religious wouldn't have been given access to the service elevators.

Conrad didn't respond, simply pressing for the seventh floor. The American pressed for the fifth, then turned and stood with his back to Conrad, his face to the doors. There hadn't been any hint of recognition in his expression, so either he wasn't with Rutherford or he hadn't connected Conrad with whatever pictures he'd seen.

But no sooner had the elevator started to move than Conrad realized it had simply been a delayed reaction. The guy was immediately edgy, perhaps wondering how to play it—a hurried assessment of Conrad's reputation and of the confined quarters in which he would have to subdue him. His right arm twitched, giving the impression that he was thinking of going for his gun. Conrad thought about doing the same, but he'd put it off too long.

The guy's elbow was suddenly and forcefully embedded into the top of Conrad's stomach. Even as Conrad felt the air being knocked out of him, he threw his left arm up and rammed the guy's head against the control panel so forcefully that the elevator shuddered with the impact.

Conrad tried to finish it quickly, throwing a punch with his right arm around the side of the guy's head, but he found it intercepted and wasn't sure how. The guy threw his whole body at him then, knocking him against the back wall. The elevator shuddered again. Conrad thought it shuddered a third time, but it wasn't the elevator, it was his own body as the guy powered a couple of quick brutal punches into his side.

This guy was strong and fast, so much so that it was overwhelming. Conrad felt a knee go up into his stomach, another wild punch to the side of his head. And all he could do was try to hunker down against it, an impossible task. They were all body blows, all finding their targets, and Conrad knew it would only take two or three more before the beating started to weaken him.

Then for one moment the world seemed to slow down around him and he saw the guy's cleanly shaven throat exposed, his Adam's apple projecting sharply. Conrad's right arm was stuck but his left was free and he threw one solid punch, hitting him directly above the collar.

The guy flew backward into the opposite corner, briefly stunned, blood streaming out of his nose from the earlier impact. Conrad pulled his gun, aimed at the guy's head, caught his terrified stare, thought of de Vries and the Southerner and Hobson. He eased his finger off the trigger and cracked the guy a couple of times across the head, the first hurting him, the second knocking him cold.

The doors opened on five and Conrad stood alert for a few seconds. As they closed again, he leaned down and took the guy's gun, putting it in the rucksack with the rest of the armory he was building there, and then tried to think what to do with him.

He let the elevator go on up to seven, checked that the corridor was clear, then dragged the guy out and into a service storeroom that was open near the elevator. He put him in the corner behind a laundry cart, but he still knew it wouldn't give him much time and, having seen the way the guy fought, Conrad couldn't imagine him being out for long. Still, he didn't need long.

The elevator was still on the seventh floor, so he dropped back to six and walked along until he found 622, the "Do

Not Disturb" sign hanging on the door handle. Actually getting into Rutherford's room wasn't something he'd thought about.

He didn't expect the man to gladly open up and let him in, and this time, not even Fox's ID would be likely to help him. Conrad had picked a couple of locks in his time, but it wasn't something he was good at, and certainly not a task he could complete without Rutherford hearing him.

The door to the room across the corridor was wedged open and he could hear the maid working in the bathroom. He stepped inside rather than standing there in the open and tried to think what his options were. One would have been to wait until Rutherford came out of his own accord, but unless he went back upstairs and killed the guy in the storeroom, he'd ruled that one out for himself.

He was still thinking through his lack of options when he heard an elevator door open farther along the corridor. He heard someone say, "Good morning" in a cheery way, and a woman responding with a slightly surprised tone—another maid perhaps.

Conrad could hear footsteps approaching, so he stood back and willed the maid in the bathroom not to come out in the next sixty seconds. A knock sounded loudly on Rutherford's door, and then the cheery voice said, "It's Mortimer, sir."

There was a pause during which Conrad pulled his gun and let it hang by his side. He heard the lock on Rutherford's door unlatch, then heard the door open. He looked around the doorframe and saw Rutherford heading back to his breakfast, Mortimer following him into the room, the door easing shut behind him.

Conrad stepped swiftly across the corridor and slipped through the closing door almost without touching it. The door eased itself shut behind him with a satisfyingly secure clunk, and there they were, just the three of them in the eye of the storm.

Rutherford was wearing a pale blue shirt and a tie and was settling back down to his breakfast table. Close up, apart from the graying brown hair, he looked pretty well unchanged as far as Conrad remembered, and had certainly worn better than Frank.

His skin was still taut over aquiline features, his physique that of someone who'd been a keen sportsman but kept trim with forty minutes on the treadmill each morning. He was around the same age as Frank but their paths had apparently diverged, only to come together again now in the manner of their deaths.

Mortimer, yet another clone with a politician's haircut, was hovering on the edge of the room. It was clear from his body language and respectful silence that Rutherford was the top of the food chain for Mortimer and his colleagues. This was probably the man whose job they all dreamed of having twenty years down the line.

Rutherford wasn't even looking up at Mortimer but was busy seasoning his eggs as he said, "So what have you got for me?"

"It's one hell of a mess, sir . . ."

Conrad was eager to hear exactly how it was one hell of a mess, but Rutherford looked up now and saw him standing by the door. To his credit, he hardly flinched, as if he'd experienced similar scenarios in trouble spots the world over. He calmly raised his hand to stop Mortimer going any further, and said, "Mortimer, I want you very carefully to take your gun and place it on the dresser to the side of you." Mortimer must have looked confused, because Rutherford persisted. "Just do as I say, and do it carefully."

Conrad took casual aim at Mortimer's back and watched as he eased the gun out of his shoulder holster and placed it on the dressing table. Mortimer didn't know he was at gunpoint but he moved as if he were surrounded by twenty armed police officers.

Once he'd got rid of the gun, he said, "I don't understand, sir. What's going on?"

"Take a seat." Rutherford was gesturing to an armchair near the bed. Mortimer walked over to it dutifully, and it was only as he sat down that he saw Conrad, a jolt of shock running through him, almost as if he were about to go for the gun he no longer had. Rutherford put his knife and fork down and said, "Mortimer, meet Conrad Hirst."

Conrad took a couple of steps forward. Mortimer looked scared but Rutherford was so relaxed that Conrad didn't quite know what to make of him. It was as if he believed there was no real danger, as if Conrad were a prodigal son returning to the fold.

"Hello, Conrad. It's been a long time."

"I wasn't aware we'd met before." It was only as he spoke that he felt a tightness in his ribs from the pounding he'd taken in the elevator.

"True, in a way," said Rutherford, smiling. "I'm Bill Rutherford, and what I should have said is, it's a pleasure to finally meet you properly. Now, why don't you put the gun down?"

"Because I'm here to kill you."

"You're kidding, of course." He sounded like Frank, simultaneously jovial and threatening. It made Conrad wonder how far the two of them had gone back. Rutherford didn't come across as a military man, but Conrad could imagine their two careers having been intertwined, each the constant by which the other had measured his progress. If Conrad had remained the Capa to Jason's Hemingway, it's how they might have been. "I gathered something was wrong for you to be acting up the way you have, but why the hell would you want to kill me?" He made it sound like a childish idea, ridiculous beyond description.

"You lied. Nine years ago in Mittenwald, you lied to me."

Suddenly serious, Rutherford said, "I lied about who I was, but I didn't trick or deceive you. I told you we wanted you to kill in exchange for an attractive remuneration, and you accepted. Remember?" Conrad stared blankly because Rutherford was speaking the truth, and there was no answer he could give. "I also told you the conditions you'd be expected to work under, and you had no problem with them at all. Which brings us here. We've kept to our side of the bargain on everything we agreed that night. So did you for nine years. For nine years you never once raised any concern about what you were doing, never questioned a contract, and then you murdered Frank, for what? For no reason at all. So you see, Conrad, you accuse me of lying and yet our agreement was clearly understood, and now you're the one in breach." With an afterthought, he added, "If anyone should be angry, it's me. But I'm not angry, Conrad. I'm just struggling to understand what it is you're seeking."

Rutherford was smart, and Conrad could imagine Mortimer sitting there thinking his boss had to be right, that Conrad was the crazed rogue agent they'd painted him to be.

"It's true that you told me all those things. The only thing you neglected to tell me was that these were political assassinations. You didn't tell me you were with the CIA and you didn't tell me I was killing for the American government."

With a touch of impatience creeping into his voice, Rutherford said, "Would it have made the slightest bit of difference? You'd have killed for anyone. You were so tightly coiled, if we hadn't given you a job, you'd have been killing innocent people in the street." He made a show of recalling an important fact, mocking as he said, "In fact, isn't that why you and I met? Hadn't you killed someone you weren't meant to kill?"

"I was sick," said Conrad, but the comment had thrown him. Was it possible that Rutherford was right, that he'd have spun out of control if there hadn't been a more regulated outlet for the demons he'd brought with him out of Yugoslavia?

"If you were sick then, you must be sick now. How else do you explain the innocent people you've killed this last week?"

Conrad could think of no response. He hadn't needed to kill Fox, he hadn't needed to kill the Southerner, and his sparing of Harrison and de Vries no longer seemed enough of a counterbalance, no longer the clear indication that he'd turned a corner.

"Perception's a funny thing, Conrad. We tell ourselves something often enough and we start to believe it. You think you were wronged, that you were some kind of damaged innocent, but are your actions of the last nine years really those of a traumatized kid? I don't think so. I'm sorry if you think we misled you, but you really need to look deep into yourself, because, quite honestly, I don't think you know who you are. You know who you think you are, maybe who you were, but none of it matches the facts, none of it matches the way you've actually lived your life."

He sounded like Frank again, an equally disturbing siren's call, but Conrad knew Rutherford was playing mind games with him. He *had* looked deep into himself, a few weeks earlier, after killing Klemperer in Chur—that was why he was here. None of it matched the facts or the way he'd lived, but he *could* still be the person he'd once been, who'd always been there, buried under the rubble, waiting for daylight and a way out.

"What do you want from me?" Rutherford looked surprised by the apparent change of conversation, so Conrad drove the point home, saying, "Why were you watching my apartment? Why did you have someone watching me in Lindau? And don't lie this time, because Fox told me you'd sent him."

"Before you killed him," suggested Rutherford.

"Yeah, before I killed him. Now give me some answers or I'll kill your friend Mortimer here."

He didn't look in Mortimer's direction but he could feel the air of increased panic from him. He probably sensed, as Conrad did, that Rutherford would be content to sacrifice Mortimer and any number of his men if it served his purposes.

Rutherford sighed, as if he felt his time was being wasted, and said wearily, "We don't want anything from you, Conrad, we just wanted to know what you were doing. I don't know, I guess it's just been bad timing on your part, but just as we realize the operation's been compromised, you seem to lose possession of your senses and kill Frank. We had to try to find out what was on your mind. That's what this last week has been about, not what *we* want, what *you* want."

"All I wanted was to quit."

Rutherford made a show of being confused as he said, "And that involved killing Frank because . . . ?"

Conrad didn't answer, knowing how ridiculous it would sound now, his fantasist's notion that there were only four people who knew about him and the things he'd done. Bizarre as it was, he didn't want Mortimer, the passive observer, thinking he was a deluded psychopath or an amateur fatally out of his depth.

"Conrad, if you want to quit, we can draw a line under all of this right now. Your contribution to the work of this agency over the last nine years has been valued highly. We'd respect any decision you came to about your own future."

Conrad didn't respond. He had no idea how he was being stitched up, but he could feel the needle threading in and out of his skin with every word that came out of Rutherford's mouth. A part of him wanted to keep the conversation going, because he knew he still hadn't heard the truth, but he knew also that he probably never would hear the complete truth from this man anyway.

Rutherford eased stealthily into the silence, saying, "There's something else I should tell you, Conrad. We've lost some good men to you in the last week, but I'm happy to vouch that these were victims of friendly fire, tragic accidents brought about by a brief collapse in the chain of command, most notably as a result of the confused loyalties of Frank Dillon."

"What do you mean, confused? Who was Frank working for?"

"Frank was a patriot, but he was complex, you knew that. After all, you know that he had a working relationship with Julius Eberhardt, a known crime boss." Conrad nodded, understanding that Rutherford was simply trying to set up a dead man. "The important point is that if you kill me, as you feel you have every right to do, and to some extent I can't blame you, there will be no one left to vouch for you, and this agency will spare no expense or resource in tracking you down and liquidating you. You're right, you deserve another chance—I just want you to understand that if you kill me, regrettably, you kill yourself."

Conrad nodded and shot him in the chest. It knocked him backward but Conrad got another shot in before his chair tipped, hitting him full in the face. Rutherford crashed to the floor, his legs kicking the breakfast table as he landed, setting everything on it into a brief clatter before the room slipped once more into early morning peace, the hum only of the air-conditioning.

He turned to Mortimer who was looking at his boss with a look of stunned bewilderment. He could tell that Conrad was staring at him but seemed reluctant to make eye contact, as if he could avert his own death by not staring it in the face. He'd seen that in a lot of people, almost as if they feared death less than the knowledge of its approach.

"I have no intention of killing you, Mortimer."

That was enough to get his attention, but he was still shell-shocked as he said, "I don't know what he said. Why . . . what made you kill him then?"

Conrad shook his head and, thinking aloud, said, "He

just seemed to be talking and talking and he wasn't saying anything." Mortimer nodded his head in understanding, and absentmindedly, as if remembering a to-do list, Conrad added, "You'll find de Vries at The Metropolitan Hotel, in the Modern Quarter. He's unharmed. When I leave here, I want you to wait ten minutes before calling anyone. If anyone tries to intercept me, if I even get the feeling you didn't wait ten minutes, I'll come back and I'll kill you. Understand?"

"I understand."

"Good."

He suddenly felt weary—all the death, all the threats, draining energy away from him, taking him further from where he wanted to be. He pulled the chair free from Rutherford's body, checked it for blood and sat down next to the breakfast table. He poured himself some coffee and sipped at it, vaguely aware of the confused and edgy Mortimer.

This was meant to be the end of it, the thing that gave him satisfaction, that freed him to go and find something resembling a life. Yet he felt nothing, only a fuzziness in his thoughts, a swarm of doubts and questions planted there by Rutherford himself. The world had shifted so violently around him, it was hardly surprising that Conrad had begun to doubt himself.

He thought back to Chur though, to the clarity he'd felt there, and he knew he'd done the right thing, maybe in the wrong way, but the right thing all the same. And he knew he could adapt and live like other people lived, if only he really could leave this behind, if only they'd let him.

Of course, Rutherford's final words had suggested otherwise. He wouldn't have given them credence if it hadn't been for the way they'd echoed the warnings given to him by

Delphine and Patrick de Vries. Maybe they would come after him, but if that was the risk, he'd rather face it head on. If they intended to kill him for what he'd done, he'd give them the opportunity to do just that and get it over with.

He stood and Mortimer jumped, bracing himself as he said, "Please . . ."

"I said I wouldn't kill you. I only set out to kill four people and I've already exceeded that quota." He checked his watch. "I want to meet your boss."

Mortimer looked confused as he said, "You just killed my boss."

"It's a complex organization, that's what everyone keeps telling me, so I'm sure you have more authority figures than Bill Rutherford. I want to meet someone who can deal, who'll understand what I have to offer them, and who can give me the assurances I need. Can you think of anyone who fits that bill?" Mortimer nodded. "Eleven o'clock in the Place d'Armes. That gives you nearly two hours. I'll be sitting on the curved stone steps. Don't let me down, Mortimer. I'm tired and I want this done with."

Conrad walked out, not even bothering to take Mortimer's gun, and headed back for the service elevator. Whatever happened from here on in, he was resigned to it, but there would be no compromise on his part. He was meeting them in the open, giving them time to prepare. Either they'd let him walk away for good or they'd kill him, and he took some comfort from the fact that there was nothing in between.

Conrad Hirst

Dear Anneke,

I've been thinking a lot recently about that first day we spent together, a day I've suspended in amber, a day I'll keep with me always. Of course, in our backward fashion we'd already got drunk and slept together at Mette's birthday party, all its pleasures only fumblingly half-remembered. And when I came to call for you that day, I remember how touchy you were, and suspicious of my intentions toward you.

You wanted—no—you insisted that I understand you weren't that kind of girl, that it wasn't the kind of thing you usually did, that under no circumstances was I to assume that one night of drunkenness meant I had a place in your affections or that there would be more to follow. The beauty of your protestations—I knew you were the one.

I told you I wasn't that kind of boy, either, and I argued that, given neither of us was that kind of person, maybe it was more than simply a night of drink-fueled passion. I thought I was a poet, such was the way you brought out my eloquence. And I told you that all I wanted was the chance to spend some time with you, a day with no expectations, like people meeting for the first time.

You stood there warily in the doorway and I could see you were wanting to believe in me. I'm Conrad, I said, and you smiled. I'm Anneke, pleased to meet you. Did we shake hands, too? Or am I just embellishing what's already a perfect memory?

It was the first proper spring day, warm enough to stroll around without a coat, to sit outside without feeling a chill, a hazy glow, promise in the air. On a day like that, it was easy to forget what had already taken place, and to ignore what we all knew was coming.

And it wasn't just us. The thing I learned in that war zone, even after I became a part of the bloodshed, is the way people who are suffering unimaginable horrors will snatch a moment of happiness wherever they can, and not in a selfish way, either. It's the misery they never want to share. Whether it's a spring morning or a little music, people want to smile with each other, to spread whatever joy they have.

In a fit of the same summer confidence, a café had set tables and chairs outside on the pavement, and we stopped there for lunch, bread and salami and salad, a bottle of wine.

When we were heading out to Yugoslavia, I'd been full of romantic ideas. It would be like the Spanish Civil War, like Paris in the '20s and '30s, a crucible of talented and interesting people. I imagined eating lunch in pavement cafés with beautiful women, drinking wine, taking pictures—that had been my fantasy.

Yet there I was doing exactly that and the fantasy had evaporated, because all I could think about was you. I lis-

tened to you talking about what you hoped to achieve there, I listened to you talking about your family back in Amsterdam, and about the family you wanted for yourself one day. I soaked up every detail of your life and pleaded for more, even as you became embarrassed for talking too much about yourself.

And in turn, you were the first person I told about my parents, and you understood and never told anyone else. In front of the others, you still ribbed me about my reasons for being in Yugoslavia, but it was always a comfort to know that you knew the full truth of my reasons for being there. And I'll never forget the night you cried as we lay together, because you realized you would never meet my mother and father.

We walked for a couple of hours after lunch that day, and came across the ruins of a large building. It was from before the war, and flowers and shrubs had already reclaimed areas of the tiled floors and colonized the broken low walls that remained. There were bees and butterflies and I took a picture of the one doorway that was still standing.

We guessed it had once been a grand building, and you joked that it was the Ministry of Deconstruction, and then got embarrassed by the joke. Your modesty embarrassed you easily. Anyway, whatever the building had once been, it became our discovery that day. It was a place of calm, around which we wandered and sat and talked. In my memory, it's as beautiful as a classical ruin—we could just as well have been in Butrint.

You sat on a wall and I took your picture. I no longer have a print, but it's forever in my mind's own darkroom. When I lowered the camera, I stared at you, mesmerized.

You were wearing khaki trousers and a red polo shirt that clung just enough, your skin was already starting to color, your blond hair pulled back.

You raised your hand and told me to listen. There was music playing in one of the nearby buildings, traveling softly toward us. I walked closer and stood in front of you as we strained to hear it. Someone was playing Leonard Cohen. We tried to identify the track and both got it simultaneously— "Take this Longing"—and we laughed at our synchronicity and we kissed.

It was only our first day and there were plenty more to come, beautiful memories, but I remember that kiss like no other, I remember the feel of your polo shirt beneath my hands and the warmth of your body through it, the soft tug of your lips on mine, the orange-blossom smell of your hair.

Why do I think so much of that day? Because it was one of those rarest of occasions, a day on which the whole world seemed to be aligned around us, when even random strangers were providing our soundtrack, as if every atom in the universe was telling us that we were meant to be together. On a day like that, it's impossible not to believe in fate.

It wasn't fate, though. It wasn't meant to be. The world was wrong. And it took me a long time to appreciate that it wasn't the cruelty of some higher force that had robbed me of you, that it was only the same random destruction that was blighting the lives and loves of all of those around us, and many more the world over.

Anneke. I've long since come to terms with the fact that I lost you. I've even tried to take comfort in the fact that I had the chance of loving you at all. And I'm trying to move on, I really am, even if I fooled myself about how easy that would be. But what I will never be able to accept, what will always hound me, even into my own death, is not the losing of you but the way I lost you. How could I? How could I ever come to terms with that?

That's it, inadequate as this has been. I have no more to say, except one last time, I love you.

Conrad

16

He collected the two lots of disks from the bank, the only things in his possession that he could bring to the table. No one from the CIA had even mentioned them, but then most of the people he'd met had been preoccupied with other things, and the rest had displayed less grasp of what was going on than he had. So he didn't know whether handing over the disks would count for anything, but he hoped they'd act as a statement of intent, if nothing else.

Then, having given them two hours, he found himself with a lot of time on his hands. He supposed he couldn't go back to his apartment, not that he had anything to go back for, other than a neutral space in which to wait. It was simultaneously liberating and distressing to realize that it wouldn't matter if he never set foot in that apartment again—everything that was vital to him was either in his rucksack or on his person.

He found a café and took a seat in the window, looking out onto the street. A friendly but silent waitress served him his coffee, and the mood across the café was one of quiet reflection, a mid-morning calm that matched his mood.

He wasn't looking at the people walking by outside, but as he finished his cup of coffee, he could feel someone staring in at him. He turned and a few feet away, an awkward-looking teenager with short red hair and pale freckled skin was standing there, his eyes fixed on Conrad.

Conrad stared back, disturbed and fascinated by the boy's resemblance to the young Serb he'd killed all those years ago, his first. If he'd been a believer in omens it would have rattled him. As it was, he just wondered what the kid was staring at, and then he realized he was staring at himself, at his own reflection.

At the same time, the kid realized he was accidentally staring at Conrad and laughed, waving an apology before walking on. His face was so open, so full of joy that it made Conrad a little sad, not for having killed that boy a decade before, but that the world could have allowed the boy to be there in the first place, that it could have allowed any of them to suffer the way they had.

He ordered a second coffee but left most of it, and even though he was still early for his own appointment, he strolled down to the Place D'Armes. It was almost as busy as a spring morning, despite the low ceiling of cloud and the cold promise of snow in the air.

There were even a few people sitting on the circular stone steps, though they were mainly young—a few teenage boys eating some kind of fast food, the hot and greasy smell of it seeping through the cold air toward him; a couple sitting together and staring blankly outward, turning to each other now and again for an absentminded kiss.

Conrad sat on the steps and checked his watch. It was

ten to eleven. None of the people he could see in the square looked suspicious, none of them looked like any of the agents he'd come across. But he knew the possibility existed that he was being watched, lined up in cross hairs from any number of vantage points around the square's confused roofline.

It was why he'd chosen this place, just as he'd chosen the exposed position of the steps, to bring their intentions out into the open. Now that he was sitting down though, he thought of all the spy films he'd seen where meetings had taken place in similarly exposed locations and he couldn't see the wisdom of it from the point of view of anyone who wanted to live.

He self-corrected his thoughts—anyone who was desperate to live. He *wanted* to live, of course he did, but at this precise moment he was happy enough to gamble his life for a bit of certainty. He had a lot to lose, but it was all in the future, not the present, and that potential loss wasn't tangible enough to trouble him; he'd already lost too much that was real.

He noticed a gray-haired man in a suit and expensive overcoat. He was large in a robust, healthy way and had the look about him of someone who ran a multinational company or a bank. Even here, in the center of Luxembourg, the amount of power he exuded made him look incongruous, and Conrad immediately guessed this was his man.

The man veered toward the steps, checking his watch as he walked, but he didn't walk directly to Conrad, choosing instead to stand a few yards away. He looked at the steps a couple of times as if deciding whether or not to sit down, but he remained standing. He looked at Conrad a couple of times, too, but made no attempt to speak. Maybe it wasn't him after all.

Someone called out a name and the man looked past Conrad, along the avenue of trees toward the Palais Municipal. A woman waved as she hurried along, laden with shopping bags. Conrad caught a whiff of the man's heavy cologne as he walked past to meet the woman halfway.

Conrad looked on as the two met and kissed, and then noticed someone approaching behind them along the avenue. She was smiling, at him he supposed, and carrying two Styrofoam cups. She was wearing a short duffel coat, beige jeans, boots, the look of someone who was off snowboarding as soon as she was done here—it suited her, bringing out the best of her youthful looks.

And despite the obvious connection, despite his suspicions in Milan, it still didn't occur to him straight away that Alice Benning, if that was her real name, was "the man," the person with the power to deal. Conrad's initial reaction was a concern that this serendipitous encounter would blow his meeting, and even as she walked around the edge of the steps and headed toward him, her smile renewed, he was only just taking in the significance of her reappearance.

Conrad was about to stand but she intercepted him, saying, "Please, don't get up. We'll only have to sit again." Before he could respond she sat on the steps next to him and held out the two cups. "I got us some hot chocolate. You choose—that way you'll know I'm not trying to drug you or anything sinister like that." Her tone was breezy, as if this were all part of some game they were playing.

He silently took one of the drinks, lifted the top and looked at it. "Is your name really Alice Benning?"

She smiled and said, "Of course, everything I told you is true."

"So you work for *The Economist*?"

"Well, everything except that. But you lied about being a computer guy, so we're even." She sipped her hot chocolate and looked out approvingly over the square. "You know, Luxembourg has the lowest homicide rate in Europe. By my reckoning, they have an average of one murder per year, or at least they did until a couple of days ago."

"Yeah, I'm sorry about that. I didn't really mean to kill anyone, except Rutherford."

It was a feeble apology, and there was no quip from her this time, just a pause followed by a carefully worded and somber response. "I think the confusion was probably our fault rather than yours. Thank you, anyway, for not killing de Vries or Harrison." Maybe he'd come further than he'd thought, albeit from a desperately low starting point, because he could already see how inappropriate it was to be thanked for not killing someone.

"Is he okay? Harrison?"

"Yes, he's fine." She looked at him and he turned to meet her gaze. In different circumstances, he could have fallen for someone like Alice Benning. Not that he could see how the circumstances would ever be different enough. "What are we doing here, Conrad? It's like you wanted to set yourself up, and I can't believe that's really what you have in mind."

Hearing her talk like that, he couldn't help but scan the square again, searching for likely agents. It was for a moment only, and then he turned back to her and said, "I wanted to make sure you understood, that I have no problem with you people. I had personal business with Frank and Rutherford, and all I want now is to quit. To prove that I have no other motives, I have something for you."

He put his cup on the step next to him and opened his rucksack. From the corner of his eye he could see Alice make a slight movement of her head, and he was certain she was signaling to someone unseen, a reassurance perhaps, making clear that she still had everything under control.

He took out the disks and handed them to her, and as he was fastening the rucksack again, he said, "The encrypted disks from Frank's place, and the duplicates of Klemperer's memoirs. I'm assuming that's what this has all been about."

She didn't answer his final point, and looked ambivalent about the value of the disks. "Frank's disks could prove interesting, though only from an historical point of view, now that it's all closed down. As for the others, I imagine your French friend might have liked to get her hands on those."

"You know about her?"

She put the disks into the pocket of her duffel coat and said, "DGSE agent, Celine Quentin, though I understand she used a different name in Lindau—Delphine something or other?" She laughed. "My goodness, you got to Lindau pretty damn quickly. Certainly gave me the slip." He didn't know whether Alice was trying to change the subject or whether she genuinely wasn't much interested in Delphine or the disks.

"Why did the French want the disks?"

She shrugged a little and said, "We understand Klemperer's memoirs would have exposed a couple of top-flight French politicians as having dealt with the Stasi and the KGB. One's still a leading figure in French national politics, the other's a major player in Brussels. Of course, with the DGSE you never know if they want the memoirs to bury them or . . ."

"So the French government killed Klemperer?"

She smiled, sensitive to Conrad's lack of knowledge, and said, "They would have done it themselves. I'm guessing one or another of the politicians took out a private contract, but you're getting to the root of things. Of the four hits you carried out this year, only two were for us. Klemperer and the guy in Madrid were both private contracts."

"Who for?"

"Anyone who had the money and the contacts, I guess. The three Fs—Frank, Freddie, and Fabio—had apparently decided a couple years back that you were an underutilized resource, that they could make a lot of money on the side."

He was confused, sensing for the first time that this was about more than his plans to retire. "Wait a second, all of this, everything that's happened this week, wasn't it all about me killing Frank?"

"Kind of," she said, in a way that suggested it wasn't about that at all. "In a way, it was about you killing Klemperer—we'd suspected for nearly a year but that was the final proof we needed. We set in motion plans to shut down the three Fs, but you moved faster than us, and we couldn't work out what was driving you. We knew you'd killed Frank and we knew you'd been to Birkenstein, though at first, Bill was the only one who understood the significance of that."

"How did you know I'd been there?"

"Tracking device on your car," she said apologetically. "Anyway, suddenly you were the priority, you were the one setting the pace, and it rattled everyone. We moved on Fabio and Freddie right away, but more than anything, we needed to know what you knew, what your plans were."

He smiled and finally sipped at his hot chocolate before

saying, "Which is why you happened to show up on the train to Milan."

"Yes." She sounded slightly embarrassed. "I wasn't particularly successful, was I? If only you'd agreed to have dinner with me, but I guess you were on to me."

"I was suspicious, on and off, not because of anything you did or said, just because you spoke to me."

She smiled and said, "I'd have spoken to you anyway. And Conrad, I want you to know I really enjoyed the journey—that wasn't an act." For some reason, her words had a touch of finality about them, as if she was consoling him for what was to come.

"Yeah, I enjoyed it. Like I said, that was part of why I was suspicious." Changing tack to something more pressing, he said, "So, if you were shutting the operation down, I take it that means you were planning to kill me, too."

"No! Honestly." She realized she'd been too insistent, and continued in a more measured tone. "The original thought was that without the three Fs you wouldn't have any contact points, no way of finding out what you'd really been doing. Without Frank and the others you would've effectively disappeared, so there was no need to remove you." Driving the point home, she added, "You know, we don't remove people just for the sake of it."

The thought that had embarrassed him earlier, his fanciful notion that only four people had known about him, embarrassed him in a different way now, because he'd clearly been groomed to believe that. His ignorance hadn't been incidental but an integral part of their operation. He'd probably survived for nine years only because he'd stayed inside the hermetically sealed bubble they'd made for him.

"That was the basis of my plan, too, that I didn't know anyone, and that no one knew me." But thinking through the implications of what Alice had said, he added, "Of course, now that I do know people, now that I know what I've done, I suppose you'll come to the conclusion that you have to kill me after all."

"Rutherford would have done," she said abruptly. He looked at her, shocked by her directness. She turned and met his gaze. "Not with the official sanction of the agency, you understand, but Bill had a lot of autonomy and he was a vengeful guy. He was grooming Hobson for the top—his golden boy—so he'd have killed you just for what you did to him."

Conrad thought of the derisive way Hobson had talked about Rutherford, perhaps not knowing he was the protégé, or perhaps trying to show his colleagues that he wasn't just some crony, that he wasn't afraid to criticize the boss.

"So who decides these things now?"

Almost like she couldn't believe her own luck, she smiled and said, "I do."

"And are you the vengeful type?"

She kept smiling but seemed to have second thoughts about something and said, "I probably haven't given you a fair impression of Bill. He was old school and he'd seen and dealt with some bad stuff in his time—that's where any mean streak came from—but he was a decent man."

"You seem to be avoiding the question," he said, not bothering to point out that it was too late to sway him on whether or not Rutherford had been a nice person. She looked puzzled, as if she'd genuinely forgotten what the question was, which he doubted. "Will you need to kill me?

I don't mind. I'm ready if the time has come. I just want to know."

"Of course not," she said, horrified by the implication. She thought for a few seconds and added in a matter-of-fact tone, "I don't see how it would achieve anything. Even if you wanted to play difficult, what could you prove without these?" She patted the disks in the pocket of her coat.

Strangely, he didn't feel much relieved. At first, he couldn't even think of anything to say, then responded with an unrelated question. "Was Rutherford telling the truth, the things he told me this morning?"

"From what I gather, yes." She left it at that but then realized that Conrad wanted more. "You know, like I said, Bill started out in the Cold War. You also have to realize that in the '90s, it wasn't easy for the CIA to . . . remove people we considered dangerous to our interests. It was even harder to remove them in Western Europe. Nevertheless, there *were* people we wanted out of the way. So Bill devised an operation in which drones would be recruited . . ."

"Drones!"

Conrad was joking and she laughed, too, as she said, "I know, not very flattering. The idea was to select people with the right psychological profile and experience, recruit them through a third party, and that way, if they ever got caught, it wouldn't lead back to us, or not in a way that anyone could prove."

"What was the psychological profile?"

"Complex. In brief, they were looking for homicidal sociopaths who were highly pliable." Conrad looked at her, and she shrugged, saying, "I've seen your file, and if it's any consolation, the person I met on the train to Milan wasn't what I was expecting."

Conrad thought back again to his reasons for wanting to kill Rutherford, because he'd made no allowance for Conrad being damaged, and now he saw that he'd been recruited specifically because of that. Their entire operation had been dependent on his inability to recover himself.

"I got better," he said. "At least, I started to, after the job in Chur, as it happens."

She put her gloved hand on his arm, a comforting touch that alarmed him almost as much as if she'd pulled a gun. "For what it's worth, I think it was a scandalous way to treat people. I only began to realize that when you mentioned Yugoslavia on the train—your file mentioned nothing about it."

"Why, what did the file say I'd been doing?"

"That you'd been involved in organized crime, drugs, and prostitution, that you'd first gotten involved while you were living in Thailand." He shook his head, impressed by how closely their lies sailed to his truth. "I can only imagine you were suffering from post-traumatic stress after coming out of Yugoslavia—it was unimaginably cruel to utilize you the way we did." She took her arm away again and sipped her chocolate.

She was the first person who'd ever mentioned post-traumatic stress and he felt bad for not disputing it, because he hadn't suffered, not on the level of the suffering he'd seen and even inflicted. He'd been sick, but the trauma had come from within and been of his own making. He should have told her that, but he remained silent and allowed her to continue.

"Anyway, apart from you, the operation was never a success. Only three people were ever recruited. One got cornered by police and shot himself, another went off his head on drugs and had to be retired within a couple of months. If it hadn't been for you, the whole thing would have been wound up, but you were remarkably reliable, and actually, if it makes you feel any better, you rid the world of some truly dreadful people, and probably saved lives in the process."

He laughed, loud enough for a few people here and there to stare in their direction. "I'd have killed the pope if you'd asked me to."

Alice laughed too, and couldn't resist saying, "Well now that you mention it, what do you have planned for the weekend?"

Conrad was still smiling as he said, "So seriously, what happens now? I walk away from here and a sniper round hits me in the back?"

She was lightly admonishing as she said, "Conrad, despite the widespread mythology, we're a highly reputable, *and* accountable, government agency. We don't do things like that."

"No, you get people like me to do them for you."

He was joking, but she looked at him and said, "I'm serious. Yes, we have to make difficult choices, and things get out of hand now and then, but we're not vengeful, not as an organization. There's no reason whatsoever for us to want you dead."

For as long as Alice talked she was convincing enough. He nodded, making clear that he believed her, and said, "Back to the same question then, what happens now?"

"That's up to you." She made a quick mental calculation. "I'll probably leave Luxembourg tomorrow. How about we have dinner tonight?"

"I told you, I'm quitting."

She looked at Conrad like he was missing something obvious. "I meant a social dinner! You know, I thought we hit it off pretty well on the train, there. I just thought it might be nice to finally have dinner now that everything's really out in the open." She looked a little sheepish as she added, "I do enjoy your company."

"Are you wearing a wire?"

"Of course not! You think I'd be asking you out on a date if people were listening in? I'd never hear the end of it." Then she qualified what she'd said. "When I say date, obviously I mean it in the loose sense of the word."

"Sure," said Conrad, though he still couldn't shake off the suspicion that this was much more than a date, that Alice was too professional and simply saw dinner as the first step toward bringing a valuable employee back into the fold.

"Even so, there might be a few raised eyebrows, me having dinner with someone who wiped out a good number of our section in the last twenty-four hours."

Giving her the benefit of the doubt on her motives, Conrad said, "Which is why this kind of thing would never work between us, because I have a past and I want to quit and you're on the way up."

She smiled and said, "It's just dinner. I want to end things on the right note. Anyway, I have a past, too." She gave him a sly smile, then stood and said, "I have to go now. How about I come by your apartment around seven?"

"Okay."

She smiled and raised a hand in a little static wave, then walked away but stopped after just a few paces and turned. "One more thing I meant to ask. Why did you decide to quit? What happened in Chur?"

"It's a long story—maybe over dinner."

She persisted, saying, "Short answer?"

He thought about it for a second and said, "I saw myself in a mirror."

She frowned and said, "I hope the long version isn't quite as cryptic." She waved again as she turned, and then he watched her walk back along the avenue of trees.

He looked around the square, looking for agents who might drift away with Alice or move in on him now that she was gone, but no one looked suspicious, no one appeared to be watching him. He sat for fifteen minutes or so, drinking his chocolate, slowly accepting that he probably wasn't under observation any more.

He was tired and wanted to go back to the apartment to sleep, even though he still wasn't convinced it was safe to go back there. But he couldn't bring himself to move off those steps. He was alone, sitting out in the middle of the Place D'Armes, and in one sense, nothing whatsoever had changed, nothing had been achieved, except perhaps that he had a date for dinner.

He felt different, too, there was no denying that, a feeling of being disembodied, of liberation. He'd created a burden for himself and had carried it for ten years. It had distorted him so much, he'd no longer known or recognized himself.

He suspected it would never leave him totally, but he knew the truth of it now—he could write it down in letters, and maybe even share it over dinner with the people he met, that they might come to know him for the man he really was.

Epilogue

THERE was something indecent about killing an old man. Conrad thought about that as he waited for Klemperer to answer the door. Surely killing someone at the end of his life, when there were fewer years being stolen, should have been less objectionable than killing a man in his youth. Yet he imagined society judged it the other way.

Maybe it was a question of fair play, the elderly usually granted immunity from violence in the same way that babies and small children were, for being frail and defenseless. Or maybe it was the notion that a person who'd reached old age deserved to live out their final years in peace. It didn't trouble him, but he sensed all the same that it wasn't the done thing.

He could hear someone approaching the other side of the door, humming lightly to himself, a man who sounded gratingly sociable. Klemperer was a talker—he'd been warned about that. During the last forty years, Klemperer had twice managed to talk would-be assassins out of killing him. One of the two had even defected, this having been back in the Cold War.

Unfortunately for the old man, the Cold War was long over, and the people he'd upset this time were from the criminal world and the killer wasn't the kind who'd be swayed by words. Conrad didn't know why Klemperer had been targeted, nor did he care, and even though killing a man of seventy-six had aroused his intellectual curiosity, there would be no quandary.

Conrad waited until the door was opening before dipping into his rucksack and taking out the gun. And as the gap presented itself, he immediately stepped through it, taking Klemperer completely by surprise. This didn't seem like a man who felt his life was in danger.

He'd obviously never been a tall man, but he looked diminutive now, his patterned alpine-style sweater somehow drawing attention to the frugal physique beneath. His features were sunken too, his thinning hair combed into a neat side-parting. His eyes were clear blue though, and so vital, so sprightly, that they looked incongruous, the only visible remnant of a past Klemperer.

Conrad shut the door quickly, but the old man's surprise had already subdued into a casual, almost cheerful, acceptance. He'd spotted the gun, but more importantly, he'd clearly taken in the significance of the leather gloves Conrad was wearing.

He threw a couple of questions at him, one in German, the other in Russian. Receiving no response, he seemed to be considering which language to try next when Conrad pointed with the gun and said, "Upstairs."

One word, but Klemperer looked stunned. "You're English," he said, as if he'd just unmasked one of his own family. "MI6? But I don't understand. Why would you?"

For a moment, Conrad felt flattered at being mistaken for

an agent from MI6. He didn't know anything about real-life spying, but the fictional romance and glamor, and perhaps even the legitimacy, the knowledge of serving some higher purpose, appealed to him, albeit fleetingly.

"I don't work for a government, I work for Julius Eberhardt."

Klemperer was no less baffled. "I don't recognize the name."

"He's a crime boss, and I don't care whether you know him or not. He wants you dead."

"Some mistake, perhaps?" His tone was casual, as if Conrad had delivered a parcel to the wrong address.

Conrad waved the gun toward the stairs again, and Klemperer nodded and walked up slowly in front of him. They stopped on the landing for a second. Conrad looked into the bedroom, saw the roof beams he'd been told to expect, and waved him in.

He'd visualized this hit in advance, the way he always did, and because he'd seen a picture of the outside of the house, he'd imagined a traditional alpine interior. But the furnishings were all modern, or at least, what had passed for modern thirty or forty years ago, a Bauhaus, retro feel to the place.

Despite the gun, Klemperer wasn't to be shot. It had to look like suicide, and the next stage was complex enough that Conrad had anticipated problems. He needn't have worried; Klemperer was resigned now, and meekly compliant, even at a loss to find his fabled eloquence.

His only attempted intervention was when Conrad pulled the rope out of his rucksack. He immediately saw what was coming and said, "I'm a Catholic, you know. I always have been, but for years . . ." Conrad carried on with what he was doing, draping the noose over Klemperer's head, throwing the other end over the beam. "I rediscovered my faith ten years ago. I consider the Bishop a good friend." Conrad took a black and tubular steel chair from the side of the room and placed it under the beam, then gestured for Klemperer to stand on it. Klemperer made direct eye contact and said, "What I mean to say is, the Bishop will know, a number of people will know, that I would never commit suicide."

Maybe he was expecting Conrad to get drawn into a discussion on what it is that makes a man kill himself. And maybe that was why they'd sent Conrad. "You're telling the wrong person. I'm told to make it look like this, so that's what I do. Now, do you need any help getting onto the chair?"

Klemperer looked at him indignantly and climbed up onto the chair. In the old man's defense, Conrad had to concede he looked pretty steady and balanced. Conrad walked across the room, pulled the loose end of the rope so that the noose tugged lightly on Klemperer's neck and then tied it to a support beam.

Klemperer eased his fingers beneath the noose and said, "You're a pawn, I hope you realize that." Conrad nodded, under no illusion as to his position in life. He walked back over to him and made ready to push the chair away, but Klemperer said urgently, "Just one more thing. Let me ask you one thing."

Conrad took a step back, smiling at what he anticipated would be an attempt at persuasion. "Go on."

Klemperer tried to ease the noose a little more as he said, "What were you told to do with the computer, the disks?" Conrad stared at him, weighing him up, realizing as he did that most people would probably describe Klemperer as sweet and vulnerable, grandfatherly perhaps. "Tell me, you were instructed to take the disks, no?"

Conrad shrugged and said, "Sure, I was told to destroy the computer. I have to send all the disks to an address in Zurich."

"So do that. You'll find the disks in the top drawer of my desk." He tried to look down at Conrad but couldn't because of the constraint of the noose. "But you will do something for me? And if I'm right, it might be protection for you also. In the bottom drawer you'll find an envelope with back-up copies of all the disks. You keep *them*. You will do that?"

"Sure, I'll do that," said Conrad, though he couldn't imagine why he'd need protection. He had the feeling Klemperer was still convinced this was a spill-over from his distant Cold War career.

"Okay, I'm ready."

It was Conrad who was taken aback this time. "You're ready to die?"

Klemperer smiled a little and said, "I don't *want* to die, but I'm ready, of course. You must always be ready, because you do not know the hour when your master comes." He looked wistful. "You do not know the hour."

Conrad tipped the chair from under him, then quickly pulled Klemperer's arms down and held them by his side to prevent him scratching at his neck. The Bishop's suspicions were one thing, but he didn't want the body to look like that of a man who'd tried to save himself from the rope.

He struggled and convulsed less than he'd expected, and once Klemperer was hanging limp, Conrad went through to the bathroom and ran the bath. He found the study downstairs, unplugged the computer tower and took it back up to the bathroom. After lowering it into the water he went back through to check on Klemperer.

The old man was dead. Conrad studied one of his hands

for a moment or two, how loose the skin was on the bone. He tried to imagine himself being like this in forty-four years, but he couldn't. He had trouble thinking about himself in the future tense at all.

He took his rucksack back down to the study, took the disks from the top drawer of the desk, and placed them in the stamped and labeled envelope he'd been given. He studied the printed address label, and thought it all slightly ridiculous, not least because he'd be traveling through Zurich on the way home, and yet Frank had insisted that the envelope be sent from Chur.

In fact, this whole job had been so tightly prescribed, he could easily believe Klemperer had been right to cast doubt on it being a criminal hit. Maybe Eberhardt had settled an old score for someone in exchange for political favors. Even so, as long as the fee ended up in Conrad's bank account, the motives were none of his business.

He opened the bottom drawer and took out an envelope which contained the duplicate disks Klemperer had talked about. He'd intended to add them to the others, but he'd already sealed the first envelope. He'd have to take them home instead, but he'd destroy them at the first opportunity. Maybe Klemperer saw the disks as security, but Conrad couldn't see past them being a potential liability, evidence of what he'd done here today.

He walked out then, through the hall, stopping to look fleetingly in the mirror as he made ready to open the door. Klemperer had probably stopped in the same way every day that he'd lived there, checking his fastidious appearance before going out into the city.

But Klemperer's image would appear in that glass no

more, nor would Conrad's. No matter how many years he had left, this was all that separated him from Klemperer, the dull-eyed stranger staring out of the mirror, a phantom that would disappear within the moment.

As soon as he stepped outside again, he took off his gloves and put them in his rucksack, then put his sunglasses on and slung the bag over his shoulder. It was sunny and warm for mid-October and there were plenty of other people like him, strolling around in the sunshine or sitting at the tables outside cafés.

He had plenty of time on his hands, so he drifted through the old town, idly noting the passing faces, almost all of them looking like fellow tourists. He came to a large irregular square, edged with cafés, the buildings tall and narrow and painted in muted pastels—pale blue, cream, pink.

He hadn't come through the square on the way to Klemperer's house and he was distracted for a moment by the city's geography—where was the station from here, the old man's house? Then he saw a face he recognized, or at least, a face that was familiar, and the city fell away completely, even though he knew it couldn't be her.

A young couple was walking toward him, the man pushing a small boy in a stroller, a healthy outdoors family, blond and lightly tanned, and the woman looked so much like Anneke that Conrad had involuntarily stopped walking. It was a blunt impact, seeing someone who looked so much like her, a reminder of everything that had been lost many years before, a glimpse of the life he might have lived with her.

And he knew it couldn't be her, but he couldn't will himself to move or to stop staring. This woman looked like Anneke as he remembered her, as a twenty-three-year-old, not ten years older as she would have been now, as she would have been if those ten years had ever had chance to touch her.

He recovered from the shock enough to start walking. Dragging his gaze from her was harder, and then it was too late, because she'd spotted him and was looking concerned, muttering a couple of words to her husband. The intensity of his stare had rattled her and that was a potentially disastrous lapse of anonymity on his part—he didn't want anyone remembering him acting strangely.

Conrad lowered his head and altered his course as much as he could without actually turning back. His heart was kicking out its beats, urging him to run, but he wouldn't run. He maintained his pace and kept his head down. He was aware of being alongside them, albeit a few yards away, then walking away from them.

"Conrad?"

He felt like he'd stumbled and fallen, as if a bullet had hit him but the pain had not yet registered. She'd called out his name across ten years and it was so familiar, so instantly recognizable, it was as if a part of his brain had remained dormant all this time, dedicated solely to awaiting the return of that voice.

"It *is* you," she said, hardly able to believe it herself. "Conrad!"

He turned and looked at her and, even though the facts had been on his side, he couldn't believe he'd doubted that it was really her. She didn't look any older at all, and he hadn't forgotten a single detail. The high cheekbones, the liveliness in her eyes, the quizzical lopsided smile she reserved for moments like this, it was all overwhelmingly familiar. He even knew exactly how her long blond hair would fall if he removed the clip that loosely held it.

She stood motionless, waiting, and then he took a tentative step toward her and she could wait no longer. She let out an astonished laugh and ran to him, throwing her arms around him, lifting her feet off the ground so that he had to hold onto her in turn to keep his balance. And even holding her, even with her breath falling hot and full of emotion on his neck, he couldn't understand how this was happening, how she could be here.

He looked up and saw the man smiling warmly, so in love with her that her happiness had instantly rubbed off on him. He turned the stroller and walked the few steps to where they were standing. The child was asleep. Anneke seemed to sense he was there and broke away now, eager to share her excitement.

"Pieter, this is Conrad, the boy I knew in Yugoslavia."

Pieter smiled enthusiastically, reaching out to shake hands as he said, "It's great to meet you, Conrad. Anneke's told me about you."

Conrad shook his hand and attempted to smile back, struggling, his thoughts in a brawl. He didn't even feel in possession of himself, as if part of him had kept walking across the square. That other Conrad Hirst was posting the disks, making for the station, and all he'd left behind was the boy who'd gone to Yugoslavia with dreams of being a war photographer, the boy who'd fallen in love with Anneke.

"You died," he said, turning to her now, knowing it wasn't true and yet unable to find any other way of expressing the quiet collapse of his world around him.

She shook her head, almost apologetically, and she looked for a moment as if the misconception of those two words had been as tragic for her as they were for him. But they could never have been, because she was standing here with a husband, a child. In truth, Conrad was the one who'd died, and his tragedy was that he was seeing it only now, that even twenty minutes earlier, killing Klemperer, he'd been completely oblivious.

"Mette died," she said quietly, sadly. "There was a mistake. But I was in the hospital. And I tried to reach you but you were missing."

Conrad started to nod, a nervous tic of a nod, acknowledging that final undeniable truth, that he'd gone missing. Pieter put his hand on Conrad's shoulder and said, "You two really need some time, I think." He turned to his wife and added, "We'll go for a walk. You and Conrad sit and have coffee. Catch up."

She smiled, full of love for him, and kissed him. She kissed the sleeping boy, too, before Pieter walked away with him. Then she pointed questioningly at the nearest café, less busy because it was shaded now, and Conrad nodded and they walked over and sat at a table away from other people.

"No camera?" He shook his head but didn't speak, and then he stared at her for so long that she laughed and put her hand on his as she said, "I never thought I'd see you again." Her eyes swelled with tears but none broke free.

The waiter came and they ordered hot chocolate. As soon as they were left alone again, Conrad said, "What happened? They told me at the house that you were killed." He felt as if someone else was asking the question, as if it couldn't be the two of them sitting here, because her death had been the foundation of his adult life, the one irrefutable truth around which everything else had grown.

Anneke looked across the square, almost as if she could see the marketplace where the shells had fallen, and said, "It was crazy. We'd bought some drinks, and the woman called after us that we'd forgotten our change. I don't know why I did it, but I handed my bag to Mette and walked back to get the change." She shrugged. "I don't remember anything after that. Not the explosions or anything. Mette was killed immediately, but they found my bag with her, my passport, so they thought it was me. We looked a little alike; you remember Mette."

They had looked alike, or at least, Anneke had always looked more Scandinavian than Dutch, and in the aftermath of an explosion, maybe that had been enough.

"What happened to you?"

"A piece of metal went in my leg—I still have a scar there—and I got a concussion, but I was lucky. For two days, they thought I was dead and they were looking for Mette. And then Nick came to the hospital because he heard they had a Scandinavian girl. You can't believe how shocked he was to see me there." He could tell she still felt some residual guilt, that Mette had died and she hadn't, a feeling intensified by the briefly mistaken identities. "They flew me back to Amsterdam, and two weeks later I was back, looking for you." She laughed a little, bashfully, and grew serious again. "Of course, you were gone. I went to your place. Jason was a mess. He'd been in touch with the British authorities, but they hadn't helped. He showed me all your things still in your room and he kept saying over and over that he didn't know what to do with them."

She was distracted for a moment as the waiter arrived with the hot chocolates, and then she looked embarrassed as she said, "I slept in your bed that night. It's crazy, I know, but I thought you'd know somehow that I was there, that you'd come back."

He thought of her lying in that dingy little room and he tried to remember the clothes and possessions he'd left there, how much of him she'd had to hold onto. It was pointless trying to recall where he would have been then; time was one of the many fundamentals that had slipped their moorings in the months after her death.

"It never occurred to me that Jason would have been worried. I don't know why—it should have."

For the briefest moment she looked angered, by his casual tone or the subtle shift of subject, but she yielded quickly and sounded almost falsely chatty as she said, "He never did become a journalist, but he's a novelist now, quite successful."

"I know." Conrad had spotted one of his books in an airport a couple of years back, a German translation, the author photo confirming that it was the same Jason Fleming. But he'd never sought out a copy in English. "Are you in touch with him?"

"Yes." That surprised him because the two of them hadn't hit if off as much as he'd hoped they would, but then with a note of sorrow, she added, "For the same reason I stayed in your bed that night. I knew you thought I was dead and I had a terrible feeling that was why you'd disappeared. If you'd had a family I'd have stayed in touch with them, but the only person I had, the only person I thought you might contact, was Jason." Conrad nodded, his thoughts hanging over the precipice, the terrifying knowledge that a single contact with Jason in that year would have changed everything.

"I don't know how I would have contacted him. Maybe if I'd had an e-mail address."

"Have you read any of his books?" Conrad shook his head. He thought of offering an explanation but could think of none. She looked perplexed, as if he'd become a stranger to her, and said, "If you'd read them you'd know that one has a character based on you, and that the same book is dedicated to C.H."

Conrad knew he should have been moved by the revelation, but could only see from a distance that it was a moving thing for Jason to have done, a tribute to a lost friend who wasn't actually worthy of it. He shook his head, ashamed as he said, "I didn't realize."

"Apparently not," she said, offering no forgiveness on Jason's behalf. "I didn't like Jason at first, but I grew to like him more and more as I realized how much he loved you. He was an only child, too, and he loved you like a brother. It makes me wonder if you deserved that kind of love."

It was a truth Conrad wasn't ready to hear, but he nodded and said, "You're right. I disappeared because you died, but I should have thought of Jason. I don't know why I never contacted him, but I should have."

He didn't sound convinced, he knew it, and she stared at him dolefully and said, "Where did you go, Conrad? What happened to you?"

How could he even begin to tell her? How could he tell her that the news of her death had sent him running broken into the night, that he'd become lost, inadvertently saved the life of a man named Lewis Jones, that he'd descended into hell with him and never quite come back? How could he tell even the bones of it without leaving her feeling it was all somehow her fault?

He'd seen the guilt Anneke still felt for having survived when Mette had died. At the moment, she was angry with him for abandoning her by default, and he'd rather she felt that anger than an unwarranted guilt for what had happened to him. She'd found a way to happiness, but it wasn't her fault that he'd failed to do the same.

He shook his head and said, "What's the point?" He waved his arm at the square, gesturing toward the absent husband and son. "You're happy, life's moved on."

"Life *has* moved on," she said, somehow implying he'd understood nothing. "Do you have a wife, a girlfriend?"

"Not at the moment," he said casually. "Why do you ask?"

"Because I didn't. For five years after you disappeared, I didn't have a boyfriend, not even a single date. I'm happier with Pieter than I ever thought I would be again, but I waited five years, Conrad—don't you think that entitles me to an answer?"

There was some tainted satisfaction in knowing that she'd waited, that as fleeting as their love had been, its significance hadn't been his delusion alone. He wouldn't tell her, either, that he could double those five years and was still counting, because it hadn't been a lost love alone that had left him barren.

"I was distraught when you died." He couldn't stop thinking of her death as a fact, as if this conversation were with a ghost, and in some respects, it might as well have been, because there would be no undoing the news of her death. "I ran and I just kept running. I feel bad about Jason, but I was twenty-two, I wanted just to get away from everything that reminded me of you and start afresh. That's it. I ran away, and as hard as it was, I got on with my life."

She seemed to believe him and her facial muscles tensed and Conrad could see that she was trying not to cry. He was still tuning back into the way she thought and wasn't certain whether she was upset for him or just in being reminded of that time.

They hadn't touched the drinks in front of them but she took a sip now and then wiped the froth from her mouth and discreetly wiped her eyes. Conrad wanted to hold and comfort her, to kiss her, even though he knew there was no way back.

Composed again, she said, "You were right to do that." And he realized that she was disappointed, that what had actually upset her was the thought of him being so easily able to get on with his life, with its implicit devaluation of the place she'd held in his heart. As horrified as she would have been by the truth of the last ten years, she'd have at least known how much she'd really meant to him.

He tried to comfort her as much as he could, saying, "If you think about it, we had no more than a few weeks together, but I was in love with you, Anneke. I thought I'd been in love before, but I hadn't even been close. That's what I ran away from that night."

He felt like running now. He understood what was happening here, how painful this was for her, too, and that life had played a cruel trick on them both. But she'd survived the shelling of the marketplace, she'd survived his disappearance, and finally, it had come good again for her, and any sting that came from meeting him here would be soothed away in the presence of her family.

As if to emphasize that truth, he saw Pieter stroll back into the far end of the square, talking dotingly to the child who was awake now. The irony for Conrad was that this chance encounter would haunt him and change him. And it wouldn't be her spirit that pursued him but his own, the spirit of someone who'd disappeared ten years ago and whose absence he was noticing only now.

"Where did you end up?"

"Sorry?"

She laughed, as if the weightier things had been put aside, and said, "You ran away, but you must live somewhere, you must *do* something. I guess you didn't become a photographer."

"No, I gave it up completely."

"That's too bad," she said, sounding detached. It was as if she'd already invested too much emotion in this conversation and was spent, wanting to remain now in the less taxing environs of the present.

"Yeah. I'm a security consultant—not as glamorous as it sounds, but it pays. I fell into it by accident, really. I live in Luxembourg."

She looked shocked, as if he'd told her that he lived just along the street from her. "You've lived in Luxembourg all this time!"

"Pretty much. Do you still live in Amsterdam?"

She nodded and said, "I don't know why I'm shocked. It's probably as far as London, but it just feels like you've been close, and I always imagined you in Asia or somewhere. You know, Jason always said you might have gone back to Thailand."

Conrad laughed, saying, "Jason knew I hated Thailand. We both couldn't wait to get out of there. That's why we went to Yugoslavia—and, of course, because we both wanted to be famous."

"The new Hemingway and Capa," she said, with a wry smile, the teasing look that had first attracted him to her.

"That was Jason's phrase. I saw myself more as the new Don McCullin."

Pieter was trying to occupy the child at a fountain in the middle of the square, but he'd seen his mother and seemed to be badgering his father to come back. Conrad nodded toward the scene and Anneke looked over and smiled.

She looked desperate for more time, as if they hadn't even begun the conversations they needed to have. But Conrad didn't want those conversations, and not just because he didn't want Anneke to know the truth of his lost decade. He didn't want to get to know her again, to become comfortable and easy with her again, he just wanted her to go back to being dead, an inviolate memory, a pain that was steady and controlled.

"Where are you staying?" Her tone was hopeful.

"I'm not. In fact, I'll have to go soon."

She picked up her bag and started rummaging through it, saying, "Give me your address, your phone number." She put a pen and a postcard on the table, then changed her mind and ripped the postcard in two before writing on one half herself. She handed it to him, saying, "This is our address in Amsterdam, phone number and e-mail."

Conrad wrote his address and number down but didn't want her e-mailing him, didn't want an electronic trace of her in his life. He handed it to her and said, "I'm not there a great deal, but I pick up my post and phone messages regularly. I never check my e-mail so there's no point giving you that."

She smiled at the last comment and studied the address as she said, "It doesn't matter. I want to write a proper letter to you. I want the space to say a lot of things, and if you like, maybe one day you'll write back."

"I'll try." She looked doubtful. "No really, I will, but it's gonna take a while for all of this to sink in."

"You're telling me," she said, and they stared at each other. And in that moment, it was as if the last vestiges of strangeness had fallen away, and he knew that she was thinking exactly the same as him, that there would be no coming to terms with this. It wouldn't just be a matter of time, because the time they needed was behind them and would never be theirs again.

He looked at his watch and said, "Look, Anneke, I really have to go."

"Haven't you got time to meet—"

He cut her off, not wanting to hear the child's name, certainly not wanting to meet him—it would all be too much psychological baggage, and he was overloaded as it was. "Another time. There'll be plenty of other times."

He smiled and they stood and held each other briefly and she whispered something, her words hot and muffled. Conrad nodded without being sure what she'd said, then waved at Pieter before turning and walking away.

He reached the edge of the square and stole a glance. He couldn't see them at the fountain and scanned the people in the square for a second, uncertain where they could have gone. Then he saw them, at the café, Pieter and Anneke holding each other in exactly the same place she and Conrad had occupied a minute or two earlier.

It wasn't meant to be. That's what she'd said, he understood now. It wasn't meant to be. He wondered if she'd have been so fatalistic had she known the whole truth. Would his descent into bloodshed have been sanctioned just as easily by invoking the hand of destiny?

Not that it mattered what Anneke would have thought of him, because meeting her had instantaneously broken down a barrier and exposed him to a critical voice he hadn't heard in ten years—his own.

It was firing questions at him now, asking him how he could have changed so radically from the boy she'd known, asking him how many people he'd killed, why he killed, why he felt nothing, and then most pressing of all, why he had no answers to any of these questions, not even the beginnings of answers.

He couldn't claim to have rediscovered his conscience or a sense of empathy. He wasn't cured, but meeting Anneke had jolted him enough to see that something was wrong, that a healthy person didn't live like this, didn't do things like this and not feel bad about it.

He'd post the disks, the Klemperer job completed, but then he needed to do some serious thinking. He'd probably never meet Anneke again, and wasn't sure that he could bear it anyway. But if they did meet he didn't want to feel like he had today, like a fragile veneer of his former self, a stranger's heart beating inside. He'd once been someone different, and he needed to know if he could ever be that person again.

As he continued on his way through the late autumn sunshine, he knew the time had come to pick up his things and walk away. He'd done it once before, many years ago in the woods where Lewis Jones had died—now, yet again, he was walking away from a dead person, in a world that was new and frightening.